TROUBLE DOWN THE CREEK

Mark R. Littleton

Chariot Books™
A Division of Cook Communications

Chariot Books™ is an imprint of David C. Cook Publishing Co.
David C. Cook Publishing Co., Elgin, Illinois 60120
David C. Cook Publishing Co., Weston, Ontario
Nova Distribution Ltd., Eastbourne, England

TROUBLE DOWN THE CREEK
© 1994 by Mark R. Littleton

Cover design by Bill Paetzold
Cover illustration by David Darrow
First printing, 1994
Printed in the United States of America
98 97 96 95 94   5 4 3 2 1

Library of Congress Cataloging-in-Publication Data

Littleton, Mark R.
      Trouble Down the Creek / Mark R. Littleton.
      p.   cm.
      Summary: While exploring Rocky Creek, a group of Christian sixth-
grade children become friends with an African American brother and sister
from the projects, and they join forces against a drug-dealing gang leader.
      ISBN 0-7814-0082-1
      [1. Christian life—Fiction. 2. Race relations—Fiction. 3. Gangs—
Fiction. 4. Afro-Americans—Fiction.] I. Title.
PZ7.L7364Ts 1994
[Fic]—dc20
                                                                  94-9220
                                                                      CIP
                                                                       AC

Contents

1
The First Trip

Everett Abels knelt tall and steadfast in the little boat. With a wet towel in his hand, curled up to make a rattail, he lashed at the water. "I'm gonna get you, DG! Better keep your head under."

Tina and Linc Watterson's backyard pool, dug deep into the ground, was the perfect place for Moby Dick battles, diving, swimming, and sunning. Linc and Tina watched the challenge match from the side of the pool and laughed as Everett slashed at the water.

"He can't stay under that long!"

The little green boat, made of plastic but big enough for

two kids to sit in and paddle around, shifted and wallowed in the blue water. Everett peered over the side. DG had gone deep, but he could still be seen. Everett just didn't know when he'd surface and try to spill the boat over.

Linc suddenly pointed, saying nothing. Tina looked and spotted DG's hand on Everett's opposite side. Everett was looking the other way. The hand pulled the side of the boat down.

Everett swung around, whirling his rattail, but it was too late. He pitched over the side, and the boat capsized.

DG shot up and out of the water like Moby Dick himself. "Got you!" he shouted, spraying water out of his mouth and wheezing. He'd been under for almost a minute.

Everett swam to the surface and shook his head. "Next time I'm using a spear!"

The boat lay capsized on the surface.

DG swam over to the ladder and pulled himself out. "Who's next?" he said.

"Me!" Tina yelled and stooped down, reaching for another of the green boats and pulling it along the apron of the pool. "All I have to do is hit your head and you're finished, right?"

"But he has to come up to the surface first," Linc said, "and that's how he always wins."

"How long can you hold your breath?" Everett asked, an admiring look in his eyes. Even he couldn't stay under longer than DG.

"My best time in the bathtub is a minute and twenty-seven seconds," DG replied. His long, curly brown hair hung down into his eyes. "But that's without moving around or any exertion."

"I bet he was under for more than a minute this time," Tina said. She clambered into the little boat and sat down. "Hand me the towel," she said to Everett.

He whipped the towel in the air above Tina's head, snapping it. It didn't touch her, but she screamed anyway. Everett laughed. "I'm good for something."

He pitched the towel to her, and Tina said, "I know the secret now. You won't get me, DG Frankl."

DG just laughed to himself and meandered down to the far end of the pool.

Tina's auburn hair shone in the sun. It wasn't wet at all, in fact, she was still completely dry . . . which made it all the sweeter for DG when he flipped her out a moment later.

"Well, I thought I could get him," she said with a shrug, when she had clambered out of the pool and pushed her dripping hair out of her eyes.

The four friends sat down on the edge of the pool and dangled their legs in the water.

No one spoke. DG was still catching his breath. Tina leaned back on her arms and let the sun warm her face. Linc slapped the towel down onto the water and drew it in, sending little rivulets out against everyone's legs.

DG suddenly broke the silence. "You know, I bet we could paddle these boats up the stream."

Everett turned to DG. "Wouldn't that be kind of dangerous?"

"How would it?" DG raised his thick eyebrows and waited for a response. When none came, he said, "We could take just two boats and go two to a boat. There are four paddles. I bet we could find some neat stuff upstream or maybe even downstream."

Linc nodded in agreement. "I bet my mom'll let us. She'd be glad to have us out of her hair for a while."

"But aren't there snakes?" Tina said.

"Black snakes, maybe," DG answered. "Garters. But I don't think there's anything poisonous, except copperheads, and I've never seen one of them down at the stream."

"They're not going to come around people anyway," Everett said.

"You never know, though," DG answered, cracking his famous crinkly grin.

"Which way would we go?" Tina asked, sitting up attentively. She wore a one-piece swim-team suit that made her look like a young Olympian. The boys all wore surfer suits with long legs almost to their knees.

"Both ways," DG answered. "I think we should try upstream first. That way we have to work going out, but when we're tired coming back we can just float along."

"What's up there?" Linc chimed in. He had balled up his beach towel and left it lying on the apron of the pool behind him.

"That's what we want to find out," DG said. "Go get

permission from your mom, and we can get going."

"This afternoon?" Tina asked with surprise.

"Why not?" DG eyeballed Everett and Linc. "Unless you guys are too tired from playing in the little pool to go after real adventures that can be had for the taking."

"No way," Linc answered, making a quick muscle and puckering it, then loosing it so that it appeared to bounce in place.

"Should we go in our bathing suits?" Everett asked.

"Why not?" DG replied. "There shouldn't be any bugs, and it's pretty warm. It's still August, you know."

Tina shook her head. "I'm wearing a shirt over mine."

"We might have to get out at certain points, though," DG said. "That's why we should go in our bathing suits."

"I'm taking a knife, too, and a belt," Linc said.

"Good idea," Everett answered. "I'll get my penknife and a canteen with some fresh water. We can't drink out of that grungy creek. I'll be ready in five minutes."

"Then let's go." DG stood and rubbed his hands as the others ran off to grab whatever they intended to bring on their adventure.

2
Upstream

Trees hung out over the creek in many places. Twice the explorers were stopped by a whole tree that had fallen over the creek, blocking their way. The first time they were able to duck under it, but the second time they had to get out and pull the little boats over the top.

Going upstream was difficult. The paddles were small and nothing like real canoe paddles; they were just broom handles with little paddles on the end.

The kids soon passed the houses that had been built up the street from Everett's and the Wattersons.' The forest blocked most of the sunlight, and in places the creek

13

looked gloomy and even a little scary.

DG and Tina took the lead, with Everett and Linc paddling behind. The forest stretched on and on. As they swished through the cool, clear water, they occasionally scraped by little sand banks covered with pebbles. Once they had to stop and hike up the stream. The water was only up to their ankles, and it ran by in a surge of white water, though it wasn't going very fast.

"Hey, look at that!" DG suddenly yelled.

Everett strained to see what he was referring to. He looked ahead and saw something looking misty and white in the sunlight, but he couldn't tell what it was.

"That has to be the biggest spider web I ever saw!" DG exclaimed.

He and Tina passed under it, and DG whipped at the web with his paddle. The spider nest fell apart in long, sticky strings.

"Yuck!" Tina said.

"Look, there's the spider," said DG. "He's a big one too." He lashed at the nest.

"What kind is it?" Everett asked. He watched DG cut at the web and tried to get under the spot where the large spider hung.

"Not a tarantula," DG said. "They don't live this far north."

"I know that," Everett said, giving Tina an exasperated look.

DG finally swatted the spider into the water, where it

14

squirmed and writhed on the surface. "I shouldn't have done that," he said. "Now it'll drown."

"So what?" said Linc. "It's a spider. He deserves to drown."

"It just so happens," DG intoned, "that spiders are an important part of the food chain. They eat flies and rid the atmosphere of all kinds of unwanted pests. Spiders are very important creatures."

"You want to take him home to sleep in your bed?" Tina said. She had gotten under the spider with the flat spatula part of the paddle. She gently lifted it and brought it up close to her face. "It's awfully hairy."

"It's a mygalomorph," DG said.

Everyone turned to look at him. "A what?"

"The largest class of spiders," DG answered matter-of-factly. He poked at the spider, and it curled its legs around its body, protecting itself. "There are 30,000 or more species in the whole world."

"How do you know that?" Tina asked, giving DG a respectful look.

"I read," DG said. His face wore a modest smile. "Don't you read?"

"Not about spiders," Tina said, putting her hands on her hips. "Nobody reads about spiders except complete nerds."

"Then I guess I'm a complete nerd." DG prodded the spider a little with the tip of a stick. "Watch. He'll clamp on the stick with his jaws, if he can get them open."

The spider, though, had curled up and looked dead.

"Fling him back into the woods and let's go," Everett said. "This gives me the creeps. I keep feeling spiders crawling up my back."

Linc made a little oo-oooooo-oo noise and tickled the back of Everett's neck with a leaf.

DG whipped the spider into the woods, then he sank back down into the boat and resumed paddling. Everett and Linc followed a few feet behind.

"Look around for new flora and fauna as we travel," DG called over his shoulder.

"What was that?" Linc asked Everett.

"I think he means plants and animals," Everett answered with a chuckle. He had already noticed several flowers he'd never seen before, but he hadn't seen anything like a new animal.

The creek narrowed in places, but the water never seemed to speed up or slow down. Once they crossed a bed of pebbles and rocks.

DG's eagle eye spotted a family of raccoons on the bank before anyone else saw them. The little coons were dining on a fish. It looked like a sucker, one of the bottom-eaters that frequented the creek. The raccoons didn't spook or run as the boats floated by, and everyone remained quiet. The little family—there were four young with the mother—just watched them with silent, ringed eyes.

When they were past the raccoons, DG navigated between a sandbar in the middle of the creek and a rotten tree lying over the bank.

Everett watched the water. He continued to be worried about snakes, though he was sure the chances of seeing one were slim. Then to his right came a splash. He swiveled around.

"What was that?" Linc asked.

"Don't know."

DG and Tina had moved about thirty feet ahead of them and weren't listening.

"Look!" Everett cried. He saw a wedge-shaped head on the surface of the water swimming directly toward them.

Linc raised his paddle to strike, but Everett said, "It's a turtle. Snapper. See the shell?"

Linc nodded. "I bet he'll bite into the handle of the paddle. Watch."

Linc set the tip of the paddle right at the head of the snapper. Immediately it snapped and gripped the dowel-shaped pole.

"Lift him out!" Everett said.

Linc raised the paddle, and the turtle held on. It was a long, alligator-knobby snapper with a short, wicked-looking tail. Both boys yelled to Tina and DG. "Look what we caught!"

DG called back, "I think he caught you. What will you do now if he won't let go?"

Linc stared fearfully at Everett.

"Snappers don't let go, boys and girls," DG continued. "You've got a problem." He turned around his boat, and he and Tina paddled back toward them.

Linc shook the paddle gingerly and then violently, but the snapper didn't let go. Its upper lip had a sharp tip and Everett shivered, thinking about having a finger caught in that mouth.

"What'll we do?" Linc said. "I can't leave the paddle here."

DG pulled up alongside the little boat. "Let's take him to shore. I'll show you what to do."

Everyone except Linc paddled to the bank and got out of their boats. Everett waited a moment, searching the ground for signs of another turtle, but he saw none. This one must have been big enough to scare all the others away. Its shell was at least six inches long.

DG rummaged through his pack. "Lay the snapper on the beach," he said.

Linc laid the turtle out flat with the tip of the paddle still in its beak.

DG pulled out a pack of matches. "This'll singe his rear end," he said. "Works every time." He lit a match.

"When did you ever singe a snapper before?" Tina asked.

"Never until now. But it works with ticks. Why shouldn't it work with snapping turtles?" DG held the little flame under the snapper's tail, and everyone stepped back. "Watch out that he doesn't catch one of your toes!"

The turtle didn't do anything for a moment, then suddenly it let go of the paddle and squirmed around in a circle till it faced DG.

"Into the boats!" he yelled.

Everyone ran. The turtle darted at them, but fortunately on land it was slower. Everett pushed off the boat just before the turtle reached him. His heart pounded wildly in his chest.

Linc laughed. "You look like you just met the wolfman!"

"I don't want to lose any toes today!" Everett answered, taking a deep breath. DG and Tina were already paddling up around the curve.

"Come on. We haven't seen the best yet, I'm sure!" DG called.

The snapper didn't follow them into the water, but it sat on the bank, its small beady eyes looking angry. Everett was glad to leave him behind. Then he remembered they'd have to pass him on the way back. "I'll be on the lookout," he muttered to himself.

They paddled along in silence and saw more spider webs, but no more snapping turtles. Finally they came around a curve and looked out upon a small lake, or at least an area where the stream collected. The creek continued draining in at the far end. The lake was shallow, and they could see the bottom, though the water was muddier.

"I think we should go back," Tina said, as they cruised out onto the middle of the lake.

"Let's sit here and eat some cupcakes," DG said, "and enjoy the silence of the woods."

Everett paddled over. He and Tina held the two boats together while DG rummaged in his pack. He drew out four

19

packs of chocolate and white cake cupcakes. "Who wants vanilla?" he said.

Tina and Linc had both turned to look at the shore, and they said nothing. Everett was turning when Tina said, "Shhhhh!"

At the side of the lake stood a tall buck. He had a small rack of antlers on his head.

"I didn't know you could see deer like that in New Jersey," Linc whispered.

"They're still around," Everett answered. "At least, one is anyway."

The deer, brown with a short white tail and a strip of black up the middle, drank at the lake. He stopped several times to eye the children, but showed no fear.

"I wish I had a gun," Linc said.

"No, you don't," Tina answered immediately. "He's too beautiful to shoot."

The four kids stared until the deer spun around and pranced off into the woods.

"We should have had a camera anyway," DG said. "This trip is one for the record books. First a snapper and now a deer. Next thing you know we'll see a bear."

"I don't think so," Everett said with a smile. "Let's get going."

"Good idea," DG said. "I hope we see that snapper again. I'd like to get his name."

"Beak," Everett said. "His name is Beak because he's got a real beak."

Soon they settled into the flow of the stream. They paddled very little, as the current pushed them along effortlessly.

Everett rested and studied the bank for other signs of life. He spotted another turtle, a little green one like the kind they have in pet stores, sunning itself on a rock.

The forest buzzed by in a glimmer of sights, sounds, and smells. The air shimmered ahead with the heat. Everett peered into the water and saw several different fish, mostly suckers and carp. Once he thought he saw a catfish under the boat and another black slimy thing he thought was an eel.

"Tomorrow we go the other way," DG said as they passed under the spider's webbing. "It might be better because there are more houses down that way. Maybe we'll run into some hobos or an alligator or something."

"I don't need any alligators," Tina answered.

It was a lazy day, and everyone felt good about the trip. Everett yawned as they reached Linc and Tina's backyard and the rope swing. They dragged the boats up on the grassy sand bank under the lip of the main bank.

When they had washed the boats off with a hose in Linc and Tina's driveway, Everett glanced up the street toward Chuck Davis's house. Chuck had once been Everett's best friend, but some problems the previous spring had led to a split. Chuck had become Everett's worst enemy, and the boys had had two fights already that summer: one between Chuck and Everett, and another between Chuck and DG.

"Holy mackerel!" Everett said.

Everyone turned to look.

"Well, what do you know!" Tina answered. "Good old Chuckie the Duckie is moving."

There was a man standing in Chuck's front yard, pounding a "For Sale" sign into the ground.

DG wiped his forehead. "I was hoping something like that would happen. I don't think there's enough room in New Castleton for us and him."

"Yeah," Everett agreed. He covered the end of the hose with his thumb and sprayed the bottom of the boat. It was slick with algae, and they had to get it cleaned off before they could put the boats back into the pool.

DG was still looking up the street toward Chuck's house. "Should we bid him a fond farewell?" he asked.

"He hasn't moved yet," Tina said, her hands on her hips. "He won't be coming around here anymore anyway."

"Yeah, we'll have to find someone else to fight," DG said, poking the boat with his toe.

"How about me?" Everett said, suddenly aiming the hose right at DG's face.

DG leaped at Everett. Stepping out of the way, Everett squirted Tina and Linc before they could run. "Got you all!"

It was an instant free-for-all, with everyone struggling to get the hose. In the end, Everett received a fair soaking too.

As they all went out back and returned to playing in the

pool, Everett wondered briefly what tomorrow's trip would bring. Who might they meet? They certainly didn't need another Chuck in their lives. Silently he threw up a prayer that their next adventure might be fun. Then he felt slightly embarrassed. Why did he pray so much all the time? DG and Linc and Tina never talked about praying.

And yet, there was something comforting about it—the opportunity to say anything to God, anywhere, anytime. He'd been learning a lot about it lately at Kairo, the church youth group meetings for sixth, seventh, and eighth graders. Everett was thinking about inviting DG, Tina, and Linc to come, but he didn't know how to go about it, or whether he even should. DG was Jewish, and Linc and Tina only went to church now and then. Everett's church was pretty conservative. Would their differing faiths conflict? He didn't want to create problems with his friends where there were none.

But still, the idea of their coming to Kairo intrigued him. It was one more thing he could include them in.

As they splashed and swam in the pool, Everett prayed about it silently, with his eyes open. He hoped it was a prayer God would answer soon. It was the middle of August already; it would be nice to get the others involved at church before life speeded up and things became more hectic.

Everett sat at the edge of the pool with his feet in the water.

Tina walked over and sat down next to him. "That was fun today."

"Yeah, I liked that snapper especially."

"It kind of scared me," she said. She fluffed her wet red hair and pulled it back from her forehead. "The deer was beautiful, though. I don't know how Linc could say he wished he'd had a gun. How could anyone shoot one of those animals?"

Everett shrugged. "I guess people think about it differently."

"Yeah. But I wish there were no guns in the world."

"Maybe one day there won't be." Everett kicked his legs gently, stirring up the water. DG and Linc were having a cannonball battle at the other end of the pool.

"Do you think it'll be hard this year?"

"What—sixth grade?" Everett gazed at Tina. She was cute, and he'd often wondered if they would ever be more than friends.

"You know . . . you hear about kids with knives and guns," Tina said. "Where we used to live, there was a shooting in our school. An eighth grader, I think."

"I don't think our community is like that," Everett said.

Tina looked away. Everett thought of saying something about the church group. He knew that was one place where kids wouldn't be playing with weapons. His heart began beating fast, though, and he felt afraid. What if she said no? What if it made her mad? He didn't know why he had such thoughts, but he couldn't say anything more.

"I'm going in for a Coke," Tina said suddenly. "Want one?"

"Sure." Everett looked away toward the creek. Tomorrow they would go downstream. He smiled. He felt like a real eighteenth-century pioneer. He knew that he and his friends were in for adventure.

3
The Other Way

With the current running briskly beneath them, the two boats slipped out into the middle of the creek and floated under the rope swing. DG was wearing a sailor cap, and he'd brought another that Linc immediately claimed. Tina and Everett were in the same boat this time, following DG and Linc.

The scenery passed in a rush. Everett didn't notice anything unusual. On the right side, it was mostly houses up a slope from the creek about a hundred yards. In several of the backyards, the kids saw above-ground pools, swing sets, and even a small Sears log cabin for kids to play in.

Soon the houses passed out of sight, and the boats

slipped by a forested area where trees grew right up to the edge of the bank.

Then up ahead, Everett noticed an open space in the trees. Sunlight shone on their faces. Everett noticed tall green spikes growing out of a marshy area next to the creek, with long, brown, pipelike things growing in the midst of the greenery.

"Cattails!" DG called. "Want to stop and get some?"

Tina nodded and looked at Everett. "I bet we could sell them for decorations and stuff. My mom uses them in arrangements."

They beached the boats and stepped into the marsh. Water and muck squished between Everett's toes. The acrid stink of skunk cabbage and stagnant water filled the air. There were trails evident through the leafy greenery; others had walked there before them.

DG tried to break off a thick brown cattail. When it didn't snap, he took out his knife and cut it.

"Dry them out and you can light them," he said.

"Yeah, they keep away bugs," Everett answered.

"But they stink pretty bad," Linc said.

"Let's get about twenty or so," DG said. "We won't need more."

The kids cut a number of the cattails and piled them in the middle of the boats. They were almost finished when from behind them, up the hill, they heard barking. It sounded like a hundred dogs in hot pursuit of something.

Everyone looked up the slope and spotted a pack of

white and brown mongrels flowing down the hill toward them.

"Into the boats, quick!" DG shouted.

The kids ran for the boats and pushed off into the stream. As they sat there about ten feet from shore—the creek was fairly wide at that point—Everett waved his hand. "There's someone with them."

An elderly man with a shotgun in his hand was following the pack toward them. Soon the dogs—there were twenty of them at least—stopped barking and sat back on their haunches, dangling long pink tongues. Some stepped into the water gingerly, but they didn't come all the way in. They didn't seem inclined to attack.

Everett watched the man draw closer and suddenly recognized him. It was Mr. Hennessee, the janitor from his church.

Mr. Hennessee shambled up to the water's edge. He wore blue jeans and a yellow T-shirt, and his shotgun hung in his right hand.

"Hello, kids," he said. "Enjoying my cattails?"

"Hi, Mr. Hennessee. It's me, Everett Abels."

Mr. Hennessee raised his hand and visored his eyes. "So it is. Come on ashore—my doggies won't hurt you."

The four kids paddled back to shore. The dogs waded in around the boats, sniffing and licking at the kids' legs.

"So you got some cattails?" Mr. Hennessee said, rubbing his chin. "Good for you. I like for people to use them. Otherwise they just dry up and fall over, come winter."

"If we sell them, can we come back for more?" DG asked. He knelt down to pet several of the dogs and let one lick his face.

"Sure, sure," Mr. Hennessee said. "So what are you up to—exploring?"

"Yeah," Everett said, feeling proud that Mr. Hennessee knew him and was being friendly. Sometimes at church the janitor seemed a little pressed for time, but he was always pleasant.

He was a tall, spindly man with deep-set blue eyes, a craggy face, and sunken cheeks. He was really old, probably in his seventies. The church had employed him for many years, Everett knew, and each year at Christmas they took a special offering for him because they couldn't pay him that much during the rest of the year.

Everett said, "We wanted to see what was down this way. Yesterday we went up the creek and saw a deer and a snapping turtle."

"That you will," Mr. Hennessee said, leaning on his staff. "Lots of deer in these woods if you watch enough. And those snappers. Make a mighty good soup. You see another one, let me know. I'll catch him and make you up a snapper soup that will hop your gizzard."

The kids all laughed, and the dogs wagged their tails happily. Everett mentally began to count them. Twenty-seven.

"How come you have so many dogs, Mr. Hennessee?" DG asked.

The old man laughed. "They're good friends, and they keep having puppies and I don't want to give them away. But I'm going to have to put a stop to it soon. They're eating me out of house and barn."

"Do they all have names?" Tina asked. She ruffled the back of a tall brown-and-white male who had to be just out of puppyhood. His whole body quivered and wagged as she pet him.

"That one's Clyde," Mr. Hennessee said. The dog whipped around and barked when he heard his name.

"And this here's Duke, Charlie, Jonesie, Sally, Jim, Lincoln . . ."

"Hey, that's my name," Linc said.

Mr. Hennessee eyed him and smiled. "That's a good name, son. Very famous person behind that one."

"I know."

"Anyway, they've all got names, though sometimes I forget 'em."

"How can you tell them apart?" Everett said, surveying the group. He could see that each was different in some way, but nearly all of them were white with a few black or brown spots.

"You hang around them long enough, you know," Mr. Hennessee said. "Well, I won't detain you. Have a good trip. But watch out for those apartments."

Everyone looked hard at Mr. Hennessee.

"What apartments?" DG asked.

"Down the line," Mr. Hennessee said. He lifted up his

shotgun and pointed down the creek. The long, shiny metal tube quivered in his hand. "It's government subsidized, and some bad characters have got in there. A shooting there a while ago, if you saw it on the news."

"Yeah," DG said suddenly. "I remember now. So that place is right on this creek, huh?"

"Right where it crosses into the main part of town. I'd be real careful." Mr. Hennessee let down his gun, and one of the dogs grabbed at it with his teeth. "All right, Bluesie, that's enough," he said, shoving the dog away.

"Well, it was good meeting you," DG said.

"I'll see you at church," Everett added.

"Yessirree," Mr. Hennessee said.

The kids pushed off from shore and climbed into the boats. A minute later, they were out of sight of the dogs and the old man.

"I hope we don't have any trouble," Everett said.

"But isn't that what we're looking for?" DG replied. "Adventure, chills, spills, thrills?"

Everett and Tina laughed.

"I think he means we hope no one gets hurt as in some of our recent episodes," Tina said.

Everett was still wearing a huge band-aid on his throat from his fall into some boards with nails in them. He'd nearly bled to death, but quick thinking on the part of DG and some others had saved him.

"We'll just be careful," Everett said quietly. But he wondered if they should keep going. They'd never faced anything as scary as a shooting.

He figured that as long as they kept to the creek, all would be well. They weren't actually going to the apartment complex, after all. They just planned to float by it on the water.

4
Under the Overpass

"Cool!" DG cried as the two boats floated along under another overpass. This was a much wider one, more like a tunnel, and their voices echoed eerily off the walls as they talked and shouted. "Look, a culvert!"

Sure enough, in the middle of the overpass underside gaped a large black hole. It was rectangular, taller than it was wide, and a drizzle of brown, smelly water dripped off the end.

"A new world to conquer!" DG exclaimed.

"A home for snakes," Tina answered. "I'm not going in there."

"Come on," DG answered. "It'll be cool." He paddled over to the concrete apron, and Linc and he stepped out of their boat. Everett and Tina followed. A moment later, they stood at the mouth of the tunnel. It was higher than any of their heads and looked cold and dreary inside. DG waved around a flashlight, letting the beam splay on the walls. He stopped the light on a large gray mound on the ceiling.

"Wasps' nest." He picked up a rock lying in the water and threw it up at the nest. It struck right in the middle, but no wasps appeared. "Deserted," he pronounced. "Come on, let's go inside."

Cool, stinky air hung around the entrance. DG stepped in, straddling the little stream of orangey clear water. Stains—gray, orange, brown—lay in strips on different levels inside the tunnel.

DG pointed the flashlight at the stains. "Those indicate how high the water rose in a flood. Look at that one." He pointed at the highest one, up at about hip level. "That must have been a real flood."

The tunnel didn't narrow as they moved along inside. They hadn't gone but twenty feet when there was a sudden fluttering above them. The cavern was filled with an echoing screeching sound and the whir of wings.

"Bats! Get down!" DG yelled.

Everett hit the ground, and Tina crouched beside him. Linc lay flat out next to the stream of water. The bats fluttered all around them, their high-pitched squeaks sounding terrible and deadly in their ears. The bats flew deeper inside the tomblike cavern, and soon their cries and wing-rushes diminished.

DG rose hesitantly. "They carry rabies," he said. "Wouldn't be good to get bitten by one of them."

Everyone stood up.

"Scared the heebie-jeebies out of me," Linc said.

"Heebie-jeebies? What are they?" Everett asked.

"They're a new diet food," DG said quickly. When no one laughed, he gave an exaggerated sigh. "You guys don't get anything." He turned around and continued in. "Come on, let's see where this goes."

They walked along single file, keeping to the right side of the stream of water. Dripping sounds filled the air, and a new smell of decayed, rotting flesh prickled Everett's nostrils. He didn't like this place, but he didn't want to chicken out either. As they moved in further and further, the light from the opening behind disappeared. Without the flashlight, they would have stood in pitch darkness.

Nothing but the sounds of dripping and the cool, pungent smells that wafted along above their heads moved in the tunnel. Everett felt sure DG would turn around any moment, when suddenly he stopped and whispered, "Quiet."

Everyone froze.

"What is it?" Tina asked in a low voice.

"Listen!"

Everett strained his ears. Then he pulled out of the air what sounded like a little rumble . . . a growly, throaty noise.

"What is it?" Tina said again.

"I don't know." DG roved the flashlight beam slowly over the walls. Up ahead and to the right was a depression in the tunnel, and a thick girder blocked their view.

"It's on the other side of that steel beam," DG whispered. He stepped forward.

The growly noise increased, followed by a high-pitched whimpering.

"It's a dog!" DG suddenly said.

Everyone crowded around behind him. He shined the light, and two golden brown eyes glowed in the dark. The dog was brown-furred and collie-faced, and Everett could see several tiny puppies trying to suck at her nipples.

"Be careful," DG said, waving everyone back. "She might attack us if she thinks we're dangerous."

DG and Everett knelt down about ten feet from the dog. DG pulled off his backpack and rummaged through it. A moment later he drew out a pack of Tastykakes . . . butterscotch cupcakes. "I bet she could use a real meal, but this is the best we can do."

The dog growled menacingly at first, but gradually the growls subsided. DG laid the cupcake out on the palm of his hand. "You shouldn't give chocolate to dogs, so it's a good thing I have these."

The dog looked away, and DG handed the flashlight to Everett, who shined it in a circle of light in front of them. DG waved the cupcake around.

"Here, doggie," he said. "We won't hurt you. You must

be hungry. Come here."

The dog moved its head back and forth as if it couldn't make a decision. Then it slowly stood and walked over, its tail wagging uncertainly. It had been lying on several pieces of cardboard, leaves, and other things it had obviously dragged into the tunnel to make a home. It took the cupcake gently off DG's hand, chewed it a few times, and swallowed. DG quickly produced a second, then a third, and the dog scarfed them up with speed and relish. The tiny puppies bumbled around on the little nest behind their mother.

Everett reached out and patted the dog's head. The animal seemed starved for affection, and soon all four of the kids were petting and caressing the dog happily. A moment later, Tina picked up one of the puppies and kissed it. There were three others, and each of the kids picked up one. The mother dog's tail wagged happily as the kids nuzzled and stroked the furry little forms.

"I wonder why she's in here," Tina said.

"A lot of dogs go off somewhere to have their puppies," DG said. "They want to be private, I guess. We had one that disappeared every year when it was puppy time. Then she'd come back with her brood in about three weeks."

"I wonder what her name is," Linc said as he knelt by the dog and hugged her. "She's real friendly. Maybe she's a stray."

"Looks like a mutt," Everett said. He was thinking about how nice it would be to have his own dog. But he knew he couldn't take this one home today. "She's got some collie in her, and Lab."

"German shepherd, too," DG said. "Definitely not a purebred."

The mother dog soon went back to her bed, and the kids released the puppies. Soon they were all sucking happily again.

"Well, I guess we've seen enough," DG said. He started to turn around, when he suddenly fell into a crouch and whispered, "Hush!" He turned off his flashlight.

Everything was thrown into darkness.

5
Intruders

Everett felt DG near him. "What is it?" he asked.

"Someone's coming."

Straining in the darkness, the kids heard scraping noises in the tunnel and then saw the end beam of a flashlight.

"Queenie!" a voice called. Male. Fairly strong. But a kid. "Hey, Queenie, girl? You there?"

Everett felt the dog brush past him. With a sudden charge of energy, she barked loudly.

"There she is!" the same voice said.

"She looks okay," another voice answered. A girl. Smaller. Younger.

No one moved. They all waited, crouching, fearful.

The dog reached the person with the flashlight and jumped up, barking. The barks echoed off the walls in loud leaps of sound.

"How ya doin,' girl? Everything okay?"

The dog turned around and padded back toward the kids. Everett could see her clearly in the beam of the boy's flashlight. Then the dog stopped, looking at the foursome. The flashlight came nearer.

"What is it, girl?" The boy raised the beam of the flashlight and leveled it right in Everett's eyes.

"Who are you?" DG said immediately.

The dog jumped back and scurried over to the boy again.

"Who are you?" the boy replied. "And what are you doing here? We saw your boats. You're not gonna take my dog, are you?"

DG stepped forward, holding out his hand. "Put down the flashlight. It's right in my eyes."

"I'll put it down when I'm good and ready. You have any weapons?"

"No."

"You here to fight?"

"No."

"Then what do you want?"

The others let DG do the talking. "We were just exploring. What's your name?"

"That's none of your business."

"Well, I'm DG Frankl. This is Everett Abels and Linc and Tina Watterson. We were just looking around. We didn't expect to find a dog and a passel of puppies in here."

The boy lowered his flashlight slowly till it shone in a circle on the concrete floor of the culvert.

"Safest place for her." The kid had a low voice, much lower than he should have had for his age. Everett figured he was in at least fifth grade, maybe sixth.

"My mom won't let me keep the dog, so I brought her here."

The little girl behind him suddenly piped up, "Tell him your name, Jesse."

"Shush." But the boy turned back to the foursome. "My name's Jesse Hawkins. I'm eleven. This is Boop, but her real name is Deanna. She's only eight." He shined the flashlight on his sister.

She was pretty, dark-skinned, with a tall straight-up braided pigtail on the top of her head.

Everyone was still for a moment, then DG said, "What did you call the dog?"

"Queenie," Jesse answered. "Haven't named the pups."

For the first time, Everett could hear a smile in the boy's voice. The dog nuzzled Jesse's hand and licked it, then padded back over to the pups and lay down.

"She's a nice dog," Everett said when everyone had lapsed once again into silence.

"Best dog ever," Jesse said abruptly. "None better. Boop and me came to give Queenie some food." He walked over to the little bed on the ground, set down a bone, and then poured some meal into a little bowl no one had noticed.

Boop grinned happily and joined her brother in the circle of light. Everett noticed that her two front teeth were missing and that Jesse had a silver tooth. Both kids looked as if they'd been roughly treated. Jesse's lip was broken in one spot, and the girl had a cut above her left eye.

"Jesse's gonna give one of the pups to me," Boop said, her eyes glittering with enthusiasm. "The littlest one. That's the one I want. Name him Michael."

"For some hero?" Everett asked.

"No, I just like the name," Boop replied, looking up at Everett.

"That's a good name," DG interrupted. "The greatest angel is named Michael."

"Yeah, he's the one that gonna blow the horn," Boop said, placing her hands behind her back.

"Well, Queenie, you're all right," Jesse said. "I guess I'm gonna go. Those are cool boats you guys got."

Everyone gave the dog another pat and then started back down the culvert.

"Do you want to go in one?" DG asked. "We can show you how it works."

"Don't have to do that for me," Jesse said.

"We want to," DG answered. He looked at Everett and Linc and Tina. "Don't we?"

"Sure," they all said.

In a couple minutes they all stepped out of the stinky air

of the culvert onto the flat concrete under the overpass. The two boats sat on the edge, just above the lapping water. A breeze grabbed at the water and pitched little waves at the fringes of the bank. DG pushed the closest boat into the creek.

"I'll get in first, and Jesse can come with me. Evvie, you take Boop. Linc and Tina, you can walk along on the bank."

"Thanks a lot," Tina said, but Everett could see she didn't mind. He stilled his boat at the edge of the water and said to Boop, "Go ahead, get in."

The two little boats slipped out into the current and began bobbing along down the stream. Linc and Tina ran along easily on the bank. There weren't many trees growing right by the creek, and there was a worn path there that others had made.

Jesse got the hang of the boat quickly and paddled perfectly in the seat behind DG. In his boat, Everett did most of the steering by paddling hard on one side and then the other, but Boop, sitting in the front, tried hard to help. The boats kept close together. Soon the tall apartment complex came into view.

"That's where I live," Jesse said. "The Lewis Projects."

"I heard there was a shooting here last week," Everett overheard DG say.

"Yeah. Guy deserved it. He was a squealer."

Everett listened to DG and Jesse talk, and found that it worried him. Jesse was definitely a classic "street kid," hardened by years in a tough neighborhood. Two kids like that came to Kairo, and they were rough characters, getting into scrapes now and then that appeared to Everett to be deadly. Still, he decided not to say anything for now. There was no immediate danger, and Jesse seemed like a nice enough kid. Anyone who loved a dog enough to hide it in a culvert and bring it food had to have some heart.

They reached the Projects and struck shore. Linc and Tina were waiting.

"We won!" Tina said.

Jesse got out, and then DG. Everett and Boop followed. Her little braided pigtail on the top of her head bobbed as she walked.

"You want to come in aways and see our place?" Jesse said, looking at the kids as if challenging them. "We don't have no white kids around here much, but I figger you might like to see where we live."

"Sure," DG said, looking at the others. The birthmark on his left cheek shone brightly in the air, and Everett could see that Jesse and Boop were looking at it when they thought DG didn't notice. The birthmark was a large red blotch splattered over DG's cheek as if he'd been hit there with a raspberry snowball. Everett was so used to it that he hardly ever noticed it, except when they ran into new people.

As if cued in that it was the right moment to ask, Jesse said, "What happened to your cheek?"

DG touched it dramatically. "I was bitten by a dinosaur."

"Get out." Jesse cracked a wide smile, and Boop laughed aloud. "You weren't bitten by no dinosaur," Jesse said. "They all dead."

"Well, actually," DG said, shifting his feet. "I was kissed there by an angel when I was in the womb."

Jesse gazed at him a moment, then grinned. "That's as good an explanation as any, I guess. You one of us for that." He held out his hand and suddenly everyone was shaking hands.

Then Jesse said, "I'll show you how to shake like one of the brothers." He then grabbed DG's hand and went through a series of finger-touching taps and squeezes that no one could follow. When he was done, Jesse said, "I'll do it slower. You can get it."

Everyone watched closely, and in a second or two DG tried to mimic it as Jesse led him through the motions. In another minute DG had it and then Jesse tried it out on Everett and finally Linc. "Don't do it with no woman," he said to Tina.

She rolled her eyes. "I didn't want to do it anyway."

Jesse patted her on the arm. "Nah, I'll show ya. I don't care if you're a girl. Got to be fair, right?"

Tina smiled with exceptional friendliness and responded to Jesse's first motion. In a moment she had it too.

"So now you know how the brothers do it. Got it?" Jesse said.

"Got it," DG answered.

Everett looked over the complex. It was brick and

concrete, a number of long four-story buildings. He thought at least a thousand people must live there, maybe more. Nothing about it looked scary, but there was a lot of graffiti on the open-walled sides of the buildings with bad words and slogans on them in black, green, yellow, and blue paint.

The end of one building, though, was covered by a beautiful mural. It pictured a boy playing checkers with an old man and a younger man standing in the middle watching. It was very well done. Everett was amazed that someone could paint a picture so big, and on the side of the building. It must have taken months.

There were lots of people in the complex area, walking around and talking.

"Come on, you can meet some of the brothers," Jesse said. He turned around, motioning for the kids to follow. They came around between two buildings, the one with the graffiti and the other with the mural. A long drive went around in front of them, and there was a park area with swings, merry-go-rounds, and other playground equipment. Kids were playing everywhere, with mothers sitting here and there on benches watching and reading. People walked to and fro.

Jesse walked along with a swagger, as if he owned the whole complex. Boop walked shyly along behind him. She kept turning around and smiling at Everett, who wasn't sure why. The foursome followed and DG quickly strode up next to Jesse, who was prancing along like some young filly in the pasture.

"You wanta play some ball?" Jesse said. "I kin organize a game real quick."

There was a baseball field down the street on the right, and some kids lolled about on the fence. They looked as though they didn't have anything to do.

As they walked along, people stopped and stared. Everett could feel their eyes on him and the others, and it scared him. People didn't even try to pretend they weren't staring. Several gave them disgusted looks, but most of the people appeared friendly. Most didn't say anything, though as they went by, they heard one man say, "What they doin' here?"

Everett just ignored it. His heart was rumbling, though, and he hoped no one noticed how scared he was. He had never been in a situation like this, with only black people around. Though his parents encouraged him to be fair about all people and to resist the nasty thoughts of prejudice that came into people's minds, still Everett was unsure what to think or do. Did these people like him? Did they wish he would go away?

He wondered what DG and Tina and Linc were thinking. But DG kept up a constant chatter with Jesse about baseball, the Phillies, who was the best pitcher and who would go to the World Series and so on. Everett was always amazed at how easily DG could fit into different situations.

They reached the baseball diamond, and one of the kids jumped off the fence. Jesse cried, "David, my man." He slapped the boy's hand with his hand and turned around. "These are my new friends." He introduced everyone around, then called the other kids. "We gonna play some ball! What you say?"

"What—them against us?" the boy named David said. He was taller than Jesse, though he didn't look older. He had a long scar on his chest that was visible through the vee in his Phillies T-shirt. He looked tough and was probably a good player.

"There's only four of them and eight of us," Jesse said, taking a quick count. "We'll just divide up."

"I'm not taking Boop," David said.

Tears came into the little girl's eyes, and Tina walked over and took her hand. "Boop and I will watch," she volunteered.

"Nah, you can both play," Jesse said. "Boop ain't that bad. Come on, me and Boop'll be with my friends here, and you guys be the other team. We's the Phillies. Who you gonna be?"

"New York, I guess," David answered. He swung around and spoke softly to the other kids gathered behind him. They were all smaller and younger, but they looked eager to play. Some of the gloves they had on looked older than themselves. Probably hand-me-downs from older brothers, Everett thought.

Jesse shot odds with David, and it was agreed that David's team would bat first. Everyone walked out onto the field. Jesse said he'd pitch. He put Everett at first and DG at short. Tina took left field—Everett knew she could catch, and he volunteered her. Boop took center. David's team had to hit to center or left. All balls in right field would be fouls.

The game began, and Jesse actually threw hardball. His pitches were fast and mean, and even Everett was glad he didn't have to bat against him. He hadn't expected fastball, but if that was what they were playing, he wasn't about to disagree.

David was up first. He had just taken up the bat when there was a shout. "Harley's coming!"

It was as if the sky had fallen. All the kids dropped their bats and gloves where they stood and ran the opposite way. The field was cleared in a minute. Boop ran in and stood with her brother, who hadn't moved off the mound. He stood there with his glove dangling. DG and Everett ran in, and Linc and Tina were right behind them. Everett had noticed a group of older kids coming up the sidewalk. They didn't look friendly.

"Who's Harley?" DG asked.

"Him," Jesse said. "Harley Spenks."

Everyone turned to look at the muscular leader of the band. He reached the low cyclone fence that surrounded the field. He wore high top sneakers and a dirty T-shirt, and his face looked a little puffy, as if he'd just eaten ten donuts and they had risen into his cheeks. He had to be at least sixteen or so.

The gang strode across the patchy grass field with

various gigs and gaits. There were five of them. One was pudgy and wore glasses, but the others looked like genuine juvenile delinquents. Everett stiffened, not sure whether to run or stand. DG and the others looked nervous. Jesse's lower lip was twitching.

Boop stood behind him, her hands cinched into his belt. She said, "If he hits you, Jess, what you gonna do? Don't let him hit me, please. Please."

The tall, gangly thug stepped in front of Jesse. "You got the money, boy?"

Jesse didn't move. His eyes were fixed on the bigger boy's, and his face looked like granite.

Everett shivered. The big boy's eyes didn't even glance at him or DG or anyone else but Jesse.

The boy's hand moved so fast, Everett almost missed it. Whack! He slapped Jesse hard on the cheek.

"You hear me, dummy!" The big kid's lip curled with anger, and Jesse's lip began bleeding where it had been broken before. His eyes glistened, but he didn't move.

"Where's the money?" Harley's voice resounded. The other thugs behind him shifted their weight from foot to foot and laughed at Jesse's obvious inability to give up whatever it was that Harley wanted.

Jesse hung his head slightly, but he returned Harley's gaze out from under his thick eyebrows. "I don't have it."

Whack! The quick, hard slap resounded again. "Where's the money, jerk? This is your last chance."

"He said he doesn't have it," DG said tensely.

Harley's eyes slowly shifted around to the little gangly kid with the huge birthmark on his face. The big kid's eyelids slit evilly, and he spit onto the ground in front of DG.

"We don't allow no white boys here."

"I was invited," DG answered.

Everett was astounded at his courage. But it was typical DG behavior.

"By who?"

"By my friends."

"And who that? These two?"

"Maybe."

Everett realized that DG didn't want to get Jesse into more trouble than he was already in.

Harley's eyes moved back to Jesse. "You got twenty-four hours, white boy lover. You don't have it then, you dead meat. You understand?"

Jesse's head moved just slightly.

"Let me hear you say yes, boy!"

"Yes."

"And don't be bringin' back no white boys here. You got that?"

"I'll bring who I—"

Whack!

The third slap rang so loud, Everett flinched. He knew it hurt. Even though Jesse's skin was a rich brown, Everett could see the red bloom on his cheek.

"You don't bring no white boys to this place again, or I

deal with them and you."

Jesse nodded. Tears slipped down his cheeks, but he didn't cry out. Harley suddenly grabbed Jesse's cheek, pinching it between his thumb and forefingers.

"You a bright boy, Jesse. Don't go ruinin' it!"

He almost lifted Jesse off the ground, then just as suddenly let go. Harley spit on the ground again at DG's feet, and turned. His little band laughed and they all headed over the fence and down the street.

Jesse wiped his tears away, but he remained silent until Boop said, "Does it hurt, Jess?"

"No!"

Immediately, he stalked off the field toward the fence. When Everett and the others followed him, he just said, "Go home. Don't come back here. This isn't your place."

Boop gave them a sorrowful look, then followed her brother up the street.

DG turned to Everett and the Wattersons. "That's not right!"

Linc answered, "No, it's not right. But I think we'd better get out of here while we can. Those guys are out for blood."

They all sped down the street toward the break in the apartments that led down to the creek. No one said anything. Everyone they passed looked angry and mean, and Everett realized how much they weren't wanted here.

When they reached the boats, pushed them out into the creek, and climbed in, DG said, "We have to help that guy."

"Yeah," Linc said. "But how?"

"I don't know," DG answered. His birthmark flamed with the anger he obviously felt. "But we'll figure out something." He looked at Everett. "What did you think?"

"I felt like I was gonna wet my pants."

Everyone began paddling against the current, and in a matter of minutes, the Projects were out of sight and the foursome well on their way home. DG kept up a constant patter of anger about Harley and his friends. "It's not fair. No one should behave like that."

DG was angry and when that happened, Everett knew, sparks were going to fly.

6
Ideas

That night Everett went to the Kairo meeting at church for sixth to eighth graders. He spotted Mr. Hennessee in the hall and asked how all the dogs were, and told him about the rest of their boat trip. He didn't mention anything about Harley, though.

Jeff Simmons, the youth pastor, led the meeting. There was some singing, a couple of funny skits, and some volleyball and basketball. After the games, Jeff led them in more singing and gave a little message about the friendship of Christ. Everett paid attention, but his mind remained fixed on the events of the day and Jesse, Boop, and Harley.

When the meeting was over, he decided to ask Jeff some

questions. His mother wasn't there yet to pick him up, so he had a little time.

Jeff was surrounded by several girls all telling him how wonderful he was. Everett just shook his head. Every girl in the group—and there were about ninety kids who came regularly—had a crush on Jeff. He wasn't married and, Everett supposed, he was handsome, so the girls always flocked around.

When Everett caught Jeff's eye, the youth leader motioned to him to come over. "I'll see you all on Sunday," Jeff said, dismissing the girls. Then he walked over to Everett and put his arm over the boy's shoulder. "What can I do for you, my man?"

"I just had a question."

"Well, shoot it out and let's have a look at it."

Jeff was easy to talk to. He never made Everett feel stupid the way other adults sometimes did.

"It's about some friends of mine. I was thinking about inviting them to Kairo."

"That's great," Jeff said. "The more the merrier, I always say. Are they Christians?"

"No. My best friend—his name is DG Frankl—is Jewish. And my other two friends—they're twins, Linc and Tina Watterson—only go to church now and then."

Jeff nodded reflectively. "That does pose a problem."

"It does?" Everett said, suddenly wishing he hadn't brought it up.

"Well, I sure don't mind if they come, and neither do

any of the other kids. But their parents will have to give them permission. And we do talk about Jesus here and encourage kids to accept Him into their lives. If your friends' parents don't believe quite the same way, they might not like it. And of course Jews don't believe in Jesus at all. In fact, many of them consider Him to be a mortal enemy."

Everett felt nervous and kept his eyes on the ground in front of him. Every time he looked up into Jeff's eyes, the youth pastor was always gazing right back at him. "Well, what should I do?"

"We do have kids in the group who are not Christians, as you know. But they're having fun here, and their parents bring them because they like the group and what goes on, and sometimes because their own churches don't have a good youth program. But we don't have any Jewish kids, that's for sure . . . though they're more than welcome."

"So what should I do?"

"Talk to them," Jeff said. "Tell them what happens here, why you like it, and why you'd like them to come. But be completely straight about it. Tell them we pray together and talk about Jesus and invite them to accept Him as their Lord and Savior. It's not heavy and not a hard sell, but if they come they'll be hearing it. If they still want to come, bring them on. But make sure they get their parents' permission. Don't sneak them in against their parents' will."

"So it's okay if I invite them?"

"That's what church is all about—bringing in those

who've never heard the message. Giving them a chance to believe and become a part of God's family."

Jeff's enthusiasm was catching, and Everett felt elated. "What if they don't want to come?"

"Well, all you can do is pray and try, Ev. You can't work miracles. That's God's department. Say, you want to pray about this right now?"

Everett lifted his chin and looked up at Jeff. The youth pastor had deep green eyes with spare, sharp eyebrows. He had a dark, shiny movie star look to him that Everett wished he had.

Jeff set his hands on Everett's shoulders. "You want to pray, or should I?"

"You go ahead." Everett wasn't used to praying with a minister around.

"All right. Lord, we pray that you'd guide Everett about these three friends of his—DG, and—who were the others?"

"Linc and Tina," Everett said with his eyes still closed.

"And Linc and Tina. Be with them, Lord, and open their hearts to Jesus, or at least to Everett's invitation. We hope they won't just say no. Give him grace as he talks to the kids about coming. And when they do come, let us all be gracious and friendly and let them all have a great time. Thanks, Lord. In Jesus' name. Amen."

Everett opened his eyes. "Thanks. But do you think it will do any good?"

"All we can do is ask, Ev. 'Ask and you will receive,'

Jesus said. So we'll just have to see what He does now that we've asked." He gave Everett a wink, then clasped his hand and squeezed it. "Good luck, fella. See you Sunday?"

"I guess." Everett saw his mother standing at the back of the gym. "Thanks, Jeff. I've gotta go." He ran off.

"What were you talking to Jeff about?" his mom asked. "I hope you aren't in trouble."

"No, Mom." Everett pulled on his coat. "I'm thinking about inviting DG and Linc and Tina to Kairo, that's all."

"Oh, that would be wonderful."

They started out of the gym toward the front doors. Everett's church was a new building. The gym was converted on Sundays to the sanctuary, but during the week it was used for sports activities. Everett thought it was a good plan.

"Do you think they'd come, Mom?" Everett suddenly asked.

"I don't know why not—unless their parents don't want them to, which I could understand. I wouldn't want you going to meetings at other churches, I suppose. But I think by now you know what you believe. If you wanted to go to one, I guess I wouldn't object. The important thing is that you feel comfortable enough to invite them. Do you?"

"Yeah, I guess. . . . yes." He looked at his mother, a little amazed. "Of course I do. I think it's great."

"Well then, what more is there to say?" His mother laughed and they walked out to their car together.

In the parking lot, Everett thought again of Jesse and

Boop. He had wanted to say something to Jeff about them, too, but he hadn't. He didn't know why. There were a few black kids in the youth group, but he didn't think any of them were from the Projects.

At home, Everett called DG right away. He was nervous enough already about inviting him, so he wanted to get it over as soon as possible. DG's mom answered, and Everett politely asked to speak to DG. A second later, he heard his friend's slightly nasal but always friendly voice.

"What's up?"

"DG," Everett said. "I was wondering if you'd . . . if you'd . . ."

"Spit it out, Abels! I'm watching my favorite TV show."

"Oh, what's that?"

"It's a PBS science special."

"Gross!"

"It's good stuff, Everett. Gives you a world perspective."

"Just what I need."

"Okay, so what's up? Hurry up, I don't want to miss anything."

"I was wondering if you'd like to come to my Kairo meeting."

"Your what?"

"Kairo. It's like a youth group."

"What—in Egypt?"

"Egypt?"

"Cairo is the capital of Egypt. I guess you wouldn't know that because you never watch decent television."

"No, it's called Kairo—with a K, not a C. I know what the capital of Egypt is, dum-dum."

"Well, I'm glad that's settled. So what is this Kairo thing? Something at church?"

"Yeah. It's run by our youth pastor. We have singing and skits and then we usually play some game—sports stuff, like bombardment, volleyball, whatever's in season I guess."

"So they try to convert you, right?"

Everett smiled wryly. DG had a way of plowing right to the target. "Yeah, I guess. But it's not mandatory."

DG laughed out loud. "Not mandatory! I'm glad of that."

"I mean, you don't have to believe what they say if you don't want to. I didn't believe everything right away. Sometimes I like to—"

"Okay, I get it. I'll have to ask my mom and dad. If they say it's okay—and they probably will—they figure I'm smart enough to deal with a bunch of mealy-mouthed Christians—"

This time Everett laughed.

"—then I'll come. I'll ask and let you know tomorrow, okay?"

"Great."

"By the way, what did you think of our little escapade today? That Harley is one nasty dude. Worse than Chuck Davis, I think."

"Yeah."

"But Jesse seems to hold his own. He's like me—he

doesn't let anyone push him around. Not too much, anyway."

"It looked to me like he got pushed around pretty bad."

"Yeah," DG answered. There was a long pause. Then he said, "We have to help them, Ev. They've got bad stuff going on over there. We can't just stick our heads in the sand about it."

"But what can we do?"

"I don't know. Not yet. But something."

Everett could imagine DG chewing his lip meditatively and squinting with his deep brown eyes and those bushy eyebrows.

"Well, when you think of something," Everett said, "let me know. But I think we better be careful. That Harley is a bad dude."

"Yeah, but brains always triumph over brawn. Remember that, Everett. Brains over brawn every time. Think like an Israeli."

Everett laughed. "That's what you always say."

"It's true."

Both boys were silent for a moment. Then DG shouted, "Uh-oh, here comes an important part. They're showing off the inside of the tanks that were in Desert Storm. I gotta go."

"See you."

Everett hung up, feeling happy and relaxed. It had been simple. What was the big deal? DG hadn't batted an eye. He wanted to come. Why hadn't Everett invited him before?

He shook his head and went down into the family room in their house. His mother looked up from some knitting.

"Time to get ready for bed, Evvie," she said.

"All right. I called DG, and he wants to come to Kairo. He just has to ask his parents."

"Well, see, there you go!"

Everett mounted the stairs and headed for his bedroom.

7
Encounters

I say we go back!" DG's hair was in his eyes, but his eyes were full of fire and so was his voice. "Jesse needs help. And we're it."

"What if that Harley guy comes after us?" Everett asked uneasily. He wanted to help Jesse too, but he was afraid this was more than any of them could handle.

Chuck Davis had been one thing. He was their age and about their size. And he was white. These kids were black. Who knew what rules they played by, if any? And there had been a shooting in that apartment complex just two weeks ago.

"It's Jesse's problem," Linc said.

They were standing down at the creek by the rope swing. It was a clear, blue sky, sunshiny-hot day. A cool breeze occasionally blew here and there by the creek, but most of the time it was just hot. It would be a hundred degrees by afternoon.

Linc went on, "I say we let Jesse handle his own problems. He seems to know what he's doing. Let's just swim, go to the tree fort, and mess around."

"He's getting beat up!" DG said. "You call that handling his own problems?"

"We can't fix it for him," Linc yelled back. "We're not God, you know!"

Everett glanced at Tina. It was uncomfortable watching DG and Linc argue. "What do you say, Tina?" he asked.

She shuffled her feet and sighed heavily. "I think he needs help. But maybe we should go to the police. Remember what happened after the fight with Chuck? The policeman said when a problem gets too big to solve, you should get help."

"We can't do that for Jesse," DG insisted. "He has to do that. And what can the police do, anyway? Give Harley a warning or something? He'd laugh it off. He's probably been in and out of jail already. He thinks the police are a joke, the president's a joke, everybody's a joke. He has to be put in his place."

"And how are we going to do that?" Linc said, fury rising into his throat.

"Okay! Okay!" Everett shouted. "We don't have to fight about this. Let's take a vote. All in favor of going back to the Projects, raise their hands."

DG raised his, eyed everyone from under those heavy eyelids, then shook his head.

"Everyone for staying out of it, raise your hand."

Linc's hand went up.

DG pounced. "You two didn't even vote!"

"I don't know what to do!" Tina cried. "I want to go, but I'm afraid. What about you, Evvie?"

Everett licked his lips and looked away. It looked as though it were all up to him. Into his mind suddenly flitted a strange question. He didn't expect it. He hadn't ever thought it before. *What do you think Jesus would do?*

Everett knew Jesus wouldn't be afraid of Harley. But Jesus was God, so He wasn't afraid of anybody. He could perform miracles. He could make Harley disappear, if He wanted. Or like in the Star Wars movies when Darth Vader just thought something, and some commander crumpled up—he supposed Jesus could do that too, though Everett was sure He wouldn't.

"What would Jesus do?" he murmured.

"What?" Tina asked, staring at him.

"Just an expression."

"What was it?"

"What would Jesus do?"

Everyone looked at him questioningly.

But suddenly DG smiled. "That's right! What would

someone who was truly good and decent and willing to help the needy do? It's obvious. Jesus would go to Jesse and offer His help at the very least. He wouldn't fight Jesse's battles for him, but He'd be there, I bet. He'd encourage him. We don't have to fight Harley or anything. That would be stupid. We just have to go to Jesse and tell him we're on his side and we'll help however we can."

There was a silence, and Everett glanced around at the others. Then he said, "So I guess we're going."

"All right!" DG yelled, clapping his hands together. Tina just smiled and nodded, and Linc shrugged. Everett knew they'd all agree in the end. It was just getting there that was hard sometimes.

In a minute they were afloat in the creek, paddling and talking and laughing. Tina was in Everett's boat again and suddenly she said to him, "How come you talk about Jesus all the time, Ev?"

Everett looked up, surprised. "I do?"

"Sometimes. You talk about Him differently from other kids. Most people just use Him as a curse word."

Everett was silent, thinking about an answer. Then he said, "I don't know. I guess I just believe in Him."

"That's cool," Tina said. "In our church we mostly talk about donating money. It gets on my dad's nerves."

"I can understand that."

A moment later, DG splashed both of them with his paddle. Soon it was a real battle.

Then things settled down, and the foursome just

watched the land as they floated by. They saw various landmarks—where they'd seen the cattails and Mr. Hennessee, the culvert where Queenie and her pups were hidden—and a gradual silence settled down over them.

Soon the apartments came into view. When the tops could be seen over the trees, DG turned around in the lead boat and said, "Let's beach the boats upstream a ways. That way no one will see them and do something to them."

"Good idea," Everett answered. They steered the boats in among the stalks of some weeds growing down by the edge and got out. DG told them to turn the boats over and cover them with leaves and weeds. The sunlight beat down upon them, and their legs felt sticky and itchy in among the weeds.

"I wonder how Queenie is," DG said when they had the boats completely hidden. He looked up the creek toward the overpass.

"She's okay," Tina said.

"How do you know?" Linc asked, examining his upper body muscles. Linc pressed weights every morning.

"I could feel it when we went by. It was peaceful."

"Oh, yeah, right," Linc answered.

Everett gave him a clip on the top of the head and pointed him toward DG, who was already making his way up the trail toward the complex.

When they had caught up, DG said, "Okay, we have to have a strategy."

"Not more war games!" Tina answered. DG was known

far and wide for his ability with weapons systems, creating them and using them. At the tree fort he had led them in constructing numerous defensive structures and weaponry that would have scared even the toughest kids once it was set in motion. "We are not here to fight, DG!"

"I know, I know," DG said, repentant. But his eyes gleamed. "But we have to be sure about what we're doing here. So first I suggest we just contact Jesse and let him know we're here, then we lie low. We don't need a run-in with Harley. Let's just find Jesse, tell him we're available, and that's it."

"Available for what?" Everett said. He kept glancing toward the building, about fifty yards away through the trees. He was sure that any second Harley would rip around the corner and grab him by the throat.

"Available for . . . for . . ." For once DG seemed to be tongue-tied. "Available to help, I guess."

"And what if Jesse tells us to go and beat up Harley and get him off his back for good?" Tina asked. "What if he says that, DG?"

"Then we do it." DG shot her his crinkly smile and shrugged. "He won't say that, I guarantee it. He knows we can't fight Harley."

"Let's just find Jesse," Everett said. "We'll worry about strategy later."

"Lie low, that's the strategy for now," DG said. "Like guerrillas. Like the SEALs in Vietnam and Desert Storm. Lie low and take him by surprise."

"We don't even know where Jesse lives," Tina said.

"Then we walk in and ask!" DG said, throwing up his arms. "It's as simple as that."

He spun around and walked toward the complex. Everyone followed. Everett's heart was pounding.

Inside the complex there were no places to lie low. It was much the same as the previous day. Kids playing here and there, adults walking around. DG walked up to a little girl jumping rope, and said, "Do you know Jesse Hawkins and his sister, Boop? I mean, Deanna?"

"Yeah."

She continued jumping rope.

"Do you know where they live?"

"Yeah."

The girl went on jumping as if the questions required only simple yes or no answers.

DG put his hands on his hips. "Can you tell me where they live?"

"Yeah."

Everyone waited. Still the girl didn't answer.

"Will you tell us, please?"

"Sure. Down there." She pointed to a door about thirty feet down. But the doors were so close together, no one was sure which one she had pointed to.

"Can you take us there?" DG finally said.

"Yeah." She stopped jumping rope and, without even a look at Everett or the others, hurried down the sidewalk.

Half a minute later, she stopped in front of a shabby-looking aluminum door. The screen on it was torn out. Some of the buildings were obviously apartments, but this was one of the small townhouses.

"Thanks," DG said.

The little girl skipped away without a word. DG mounted the steps to the door. He opened the screen door and rapped hard on the inner door. Little flakes of paint fell off and floated down the front like confetti.

When no one answered, he rapped again.

After nearly a minute of rapping, the door cracked open. A woman in a blue velour robe, her hair disheveled, answered. "Yeah?"

"Uh, ma'am, I'm DG Frankl and these are my friends—"

She started to shut the door, but DG stopped it with his right hand. "Please, ma'am. We're looking for Jesse and Boo—I mean, Deanna. Are they here?"

"They're out playin,' " She shut the door abruptly.

"Friendly lady," DG said as he turned around. Several kids up and down the sidewalk were staring at the foursome as though they were extraterrestrials. DG waved. "Hi! Anyone know where Jesse and his sister are?"

No one answered. It was as if they were all afraid to speak. The little girl who had shown them the house had gone back to her strip of sidewalk and stood there. She wasn't jumping rope anymore.

"Why does everyone act like they never saw us whities before?" DG whispered to the others.

"I don't think they want us stepping on their turf," Everett answered. His heart was still pounding, though not as bad as earlier.

"We're just visiting," DG said. He waved again to two little kids who were playing with trucks and little cars about thirty feet down from the Hawkinses' house. "Someone must know where Jesse went. I don't think we should cruise all around here looking. It might really make people mad."

Everett nodded. He kept his eyes peeled for signs of Harley and his nasty friends, but as he looked up and down the street, he saw no one of that description. They saw a lady walking with grocery bags in her arms and a man smoking a cigarette, but mostly they saw kids out playing.

"Maybe Jesse went to visit Queenie," Tina volunteered. "We probably should have stopped there on our way down. He must visit her at least once or twice a day, don't you think?"

No one seemed sure of what to do.

"All right," DG said. "Let's go up and see if he's with Queenie."

They all started back up the sidewalk toward the break that led down to the creek. "We don't have to go in the boats," DG commented. "We can just walk up along the trail. It's not too far."

They reached the opening between the apartments and started down toward the creek. The forest grew right up to the back of the apartments, so in a moment they were walking through the woods to the trail. Birds chirped here and there. Squirrels careened about looking for nuts. A crow cawed overhead. Everett noticed that his armpits were wet. The day was growing hotter.

They ambled up the trail, stopped a moment to make sure the boats were secure, then continued along the bank. DG led with Everett behind him, then Tina and Linc. They came to the bend that went back up through the overpass where Queenie was hidden.

When they came around some trees, DG suddenly stopped and held up his hand. "Voices!" he whispered. He indicated to everyone to crouch.

The others crowded around him and peeked out from behind the copse of saplings. They couldn't see anyone, but they heard the sound of muffled voices.

Everett couldn't understand any words.

"Where are they?" Linc asked.

"In the woods," DG answered. He raised himself out of a crouch and peered through the leafy greenery. "Be real quiet and watch where you step!"

They all crept around the saplings. There was no trail into the woods, but only ferns and tiny seedlings grew in the areas between the trees. Rotted logs had fallen here and there, and the stump of a huge tree stood in the area before them like a tiny craggy mountain.

"They're on the other side of that stump," DG whispered. "Let's creep up to it and see if we can see them."

There was plenty of cover. Everett felt his heart pattering again and wished it would stop giving him such anxiety. Why did he have to be so afraid? It might only be kids, anyway.

They sneaked up behind the stump, keeping it between them and the voices. When they reached it, Everett craned his neck around the right side, while DG took the left. When Everett stuck his head out, his heart almost stopped. There in a little clearing about thirty feet away were Harley and his fellow thugs with a man Everett had never seen before.

Everett immediately pulled his head back.

"What is it?" Tina asked.

"Harley and his gang with some man," Everett answered.

DG was still looking on his side.

The voices were clearer now.

"I tell you, I got it under control," Harley was saying to the bigger man. "It's a piece of cake."

"You don't know what you're doin'," the man answered. "I haven't seen you produce nothin' yet."

"I will. Guaranteed. There's a lot of money here. Easy pickin's. Kids'll steal it from their moms' pocketbooks if they have to. Just you see."

"When I'm seein' a thousand a week, that's when I start lettin' my eyes bug a little. You guys are small time."

There was the crack of a stick as the man started to walk away. Harley followed him. Everett watched, just peeking out from the side of the stump.

"I'm tellin' you," Harley said, "we can get the job done.

Just give me a month. That's all I ask."

"You guys are small time. I shouldn't even be messin' with you." The man stopped. He wore sunglasses, the wraparound kind, and his head was bald and shiny in the sunlight. He wore a leather vest over a net T-shirt and sported a pencil-thin mustache. He looked like the type of person who would carry a gun. Everett shivered just looking at him.

Harley pleaded, "We can do it. I swear. Gimme a month, three weeks. That's all I need."

"School be startin' by then," the man said. "Kids'll be hearing all the school stuff. They not as easy to get into it then."

"We can do it!" Harley almost shouted.

The man snorted. "All right. One month. But I better see some real action or I'm out."

He turned on his heel and strode away. For the first time, Everett noticed a burned-out house up the woods a way and watched as the man walked by it on his way out.

Harley and his friends were silent till the man was gone. Then one of them said, "We shouldn't be doin' this, Harley. My pop would kill me if he knew."

"Everyone's got to make a living," Harley said. "You want out, you can get out. I don't want no cowards in my gang."

"But this gonna bring down the cops again," the same boy said. The others didn't appear to be supporting him.

"Who's in?" Harley suddenly said.

The other three shuffled their feet in the leaves. Everett held his breath as he waited for their replies.

"Count me in," one of the others said.

Two more quickly followed. Then the lone dissenter said with bowed head, "I get into trouble for this, gonna be my last time. I be dead after this."

"So you in?"

"Yeah."

"All right. We all agreed. Let's get movin'."

Harley turned and started walking. Right toward the stump.

8
Danger Zone

Everett froze against the back of the stump. He looked
wildly at DG, then at Linc and Tina, waiting for someone
to tell them what to do. DG looked as frightened as Everett
felt. They all instinctively nestled closer to the stump, as if
they could become a part of it.

As the fear got its grip, Everett suddenly prayed in his
mind, "Please, Lord, don't let them see us."

DG motioned to everyone to move around the stump so
that as the gang went by they could circle it.

But there just wasn't enough stump. They'd be seen for
sure. Everett gave DG a helpless look.

DG mouthed the words, "Keep moving."

But Everett would be seen, he knew, if he went out any further. Harley and his fellow thugs were less than twenty feet away.

Everett, almost without thinking, prayed again. Just the words, "Please, Lord," came into his mind. Harley would see them any second. DG flattened onto the ground. So did Tina and Linc. Everett closed his eyes as if his not seeing meant he couldn't be seen.

Then, as if on cue, there was a loud noise on the other side of the clearing—a crack like a tree breaking.

Harley stopped. "What was that?"

His gang swiveled around. "Came from out there behind us, Har," one of the gang members said.

Harley spun. "Let's go see what it was. We don't need nobody eavesdropping on our conversation here."

They all turned and hurried back in the direction the sound had come from. Everett's heart was right in his mouth. The pounding seemed to go right through his temples.

When Harley and his friends had reached the other side of the clearing, DG whispered, "Let's get going the other way fast. We don't need them coming back this way after they find out what the sound was."

They all hurried back out, still in a crouch, keeping as quiet as they could. When they reached the trail by the creek, they started back up toward the overpass. But behind them they heard a voice.

"Hey, DG and everybody! It's me, Jesse!"

They all turned. Sure enough it was Jesse, with Queenie on a rope behind him. But where were the pups?

A second later, Boop came around the corner with a box in her arms.

The kids all ran up. Tina gave Queenie a quick caress. Everyone looked into the box at the four pups. Boop set it down so they could get a better look.

"I'm gonna hafta sell them," Jesse said sadly.

"Except the one for me," Boop answered quickly.

"Yeah, except that one," Jesse replied.

Tina picked up one of the pups and ruffled the knot of hair on its head. Then Everett and Linc each picked up one, and Boop took hers into her arms.

"That is, if Mom'll let her keep him," Jesse said.

"She will," Boop answered.

Queenie didn't seem to mind about everyone picking up and loving her little ones. She simply sat down and let her long pink tongue flap out. Everett sat down next to her with the pup and petted her a little, but she didn't show much interest.

"Who you going to sell them to?" DG asked, when everyone had settled down and put the puppies back into the box. Everett took the box from Boop, and they started down the trail toward the complex.

"I don't know," Jesse said. "Anyone who's interested, I guess. But I don't think you guys better come into the apartment area. Harley's one mean dude. No tellin' what he'd do to you all if he catches you there again."

DG told Jesse what they'd seen in the woods. "What's he doing with that man?" he asked. "Is it drugs or something else?"

"It's drugs," Jesse said. "He's talked to me about it. I stay away. That's part of why I'm paying the ten dollars a week. He threatened me that if I don't buy the drugs, I have to buy protection. He's makin' me pay him not to let any of our family get hurt. I s'posed it was him gonna do the hurtin', but you can't question these things with him around. You just does what you need to do to get by."

"But if it's drugs," DG said, "we could nail him. If we get the police involved, they would arrest him for dealing drugs. That would get rid of the problem altogether."

"I know you mean well, DG," Jesse said, nodding, "but these guys are smart. They not gonna get caught real easy, if you know what I mean. And if we do rat on them, chances are Harley'll get out of jail soon and come after us anyway. So it's bad business all around."

The apartment complex loomed up before them. When they stepped out of the woods, they saw no one playing or walking behind the buildings. Everett set down the box and Queenie shambled over and sniffed each of the puppies. Then she sat back on her haunches and gave herself a vigorous scratch with her back leg.

"Why don't you take the pups up to our street, Jesse?" Everett suddenly said. He was thinking about where they might sell them and thought Jesse would get a better price in that area rather than his own. Also, he was thinking he might talk his own mom into buying one. They had discussed it once recently, and everyone in the family agreed they needed to think about getting a family pet. His little brother wanted a hamster, but everyone said that wasn't like a dog or cat. His sister wanted a cat, but his dad said a dog was a lot more fun. Everett had voted for a dog too. But no one had said anything yet about buying one.

Jesse said, "I was thinking about takin' them out of our neighborhood. Wouldn't be good for Harley to see me makin' a little money. But then . . ."

Everyone waited on his next word, but when Jesse said nothing more, DG broke in. "Then what?"

"Well, I'm black. You live in the white neighborhood. Some people don't like black folk comin' around like that sellin' things. You know what I mean."

"There are black people in our neighborhood," DG said. "There's the people down my street on the corner, and I think there's a family on your street too, Everett."

Linc and Tina nodded. "Yeah, they have little kids. I haven't met them though," Tina said. "They just moved in about a month ago."

"So that settles it," DG said. "You're coming down our way to sell those dogs."

"When do you want to do it?" Jesse asked.

"How about this afternoon?" Everett said. "I'd like to show them to my mom and dad. We've been talking about getting a dog."

"You might buy one?"

"Sure," Everett answered. He hoped he wasn't out of line on that, but the pups were cute. And Queenie seemed like a well-behaved, well-trained dog. So if the pups were anything like her, it was a guaranteed hit.

"Then let's do it," Jesse said.

"We can go up in the boats, too," DG exclaimed. "Linc and Tina have two more at their house. Why don't we come back after lunch with them, and we can all go right up the creek."

"Great," Jesse agreed. "See you later."

9
An Auction

That afternoon, they loaded the puppies in one boat with Everett. Queenie went in another boat with DG. Jesse and Tina went in the third boat and Linc and Boop in the fourth. It looked like a little flotilla when they were all on the water.

"The Spanish Armada," DG proclaimed.

"But remember, the English wiped them out," Everett answered after DG gave a big speech about how strong the Armada had been. "We learned that in fifth grade."

"But what year was it?" DG asked.

"Last year," Everett said with a grin, knowing very well

that DG meant the defeat of the Spanish Armada.

"No, when did the Armada go down to the bottom of the sea?"

Everett crinkled his brow, trying to remember. There had been a lot of names and dates in fifth grade, and it was hard to remember most of them. Besides, outthinking and outremembering DG was impossible. "Fifteen hundred something," he said finally.

"1588 to be exact. August. The British under the command of Baron Howard of Effingham sank a number of the Spanish ships and forced them to go north, out of the English Channel and around Scotland and Ireland. The Spanish lost many more ships on the journey, and naval warfare was forever changed."

"How come?" Jesse said suddenly, breaking in.

"The Spanish philosophy was to haul in close to the enemy," DG explained. "Come alongside and then board the ship and fight hand-to-hand with soldiers. Their ships were huge and slow for that reason, and their cannons were short-range and not arranged in tiers on the broadside. You've heard of a 'broadside?' That's when all the cannons would fire simultaneously, devastating the enemy's ship. But the British ships had lighter, long-range cannons, and their ships were faster. So they zoomed in and out and around the Spanish, firing at will and wiping them out. In the end, the British realized that their secret was the sea, and forever after they have largely been a sea power."

"DG's the local genius," Everett explained as he paddled

along beside Jesse and Tina.

"I can see that," Jesse said. "What else does he know?"

"Everything," Tina mused. "Don't ask him anything and you'll be happy for the rest of your life. But ask him something and it's over for the next hour."

"Oh, come on, it's not that bad," Everett said, joking. He looked at DG. His friend's face had gone slightly crimson, but Everett could see he was enjoying it. "He'll just go on for fifteen minutes, and by then you're asleep, so who cares about the rest?"

Jesse laughed. For the first time, Boop spoke up. "I think he's smart."

"Well, he is," Linc chimed in. "Too smart. He needs to take dumb pills in the morning so he'll be like the rest of us."

"Our mom says doing well in school is real important," Boop added. She wasn't wearing a braid on the top of her head today, but had her hair combed back in barrettes.

They paddled on in silence for several minutes and passed under the overpass. Queenie looked up at the culvert as if remembering that it had been her home. The air smelled of the creek water, which was brown and shallow. Algae hung here and there in pools.

"Maybe we ought to stop and see if Mr. Hennessee would buy a pup or two," Tina said as they came up on the cattails.

"He has enough dogs," Linc answered.

"Who's Mr. Hennessee?" Boop asked.

Linc explained about the church janitor who was also a

farmer. "He really loves dogs, I think."

"Yeah, but would he pay for some more?" Jesse asked.

"Don't worry, we'll find people," DG said. "I know how to sell dogs."

"You do?" everyone answered as if cued.

"Definitely," DG said, raising his thick brown eyebrows with confidence. "Our dog had pups, and I got rid of all of them."

"Got rid of them?" Boop said.

"Sold them," DG said. "I made a hundred bucks. Course, my mom made me put it into my college fund. But a hundred bucks is a hundred bucks."

Jesse's face looked sad. "Yeah," he said, "but whatever I make is just gonna go to Harley and his thugs."

"We're gonna take care of that, too," DG exclaimed. "You watch. Hey, look, there's a snapper."

Everyone turned to peer into the water. Sure enough, a little dark green head poked above the ripples in the stream. It was swimming toward them. Everett lifted his paddle out of the water and shook it in front of the snapper's snout.

"It's a small one," DG said. "Want to catch him?"

"With what?" Tina asked. She was closest now. The four boats had gathered together, and the snapper was in the center of them.

"Watch that he doesn't dive," Everett said. He tried to get under the snapper with his paddle. "I bet I can lift him out." At that moment, he jerked his paddle up under the snapper. The turtle came up on it, but quickly scurried off the edge and dived back in.

"He's gone now!" Tina shouted. "He better not be coming this way."

A moment later, the snapper's head burst up on the other side of the boats.

"He's making time," Jesse said with a laugh. "He gonna be gone now. Don't want none of your type cooping him up in a box somewhere."

"Next time we come down this way, we're bringing the right equipment," DG said as they all began paddling again up the creek. Going against the current was slow, but they still made headway.

The cattails soon disappeared behind them, and they started up toward home. When they reached Linc and Tina's backyard, they beached the boats. Jesse looked up toward the house in amazement. "You got a pool? In the ground and everything?"

"Yeah," Tina said. "You and Boop can come and swim in it."

"I'm right there!" Jesse exclaimed.

Boop was still staring up the hill. "I never seen a real home pool like that," she said.

DG set the box of puppies on the ground. Queenie walked over and inspected them, but after a sniff she lay down and rolled on the lawn.

"She itching her back," Jesse said. "Always does it."

"I hope she doesn't have fleas," Tina said.

"She got 'em," Jesse said. "That's why my mom kicked her out. I don't know what to do."

"Flea bath, here we come," DG said. He picked up the puppies. "Come on, we've got to sell these little dog burgers today. Forget the fleas for now. We'll get Queenie a flea collar with the money we make."

They all started up the hill. Jesse led Queenie on the rope leash. She followed obediently, swishing her long, stringy-haired tail happily. Tina walked with Boop, holding her hand. Linc and Everett brought up the rear.

Everett was thinking about taking them over to his house first, since he hoped his mom would take one of the pups. But if she didn't, he was afraid everyone would be disappointed. He decided to hold back till they saw how it went on the street.

"Okay, now here's the strategy," DG said when they reached the street. "First we make the dogs look their best. We need bows for the tails of the girl dogs, and little collars and stuff for all of them. Then we go for the kids. Get the kids hopped up about a puppy, and Mom and Dad follow. Understand?"

"Sounds good to me," Jesse said. "How much you think we should ask for them?"

"Fifty?" Tina suggested.

"Fifty dollars?" DG answered. "No way. Let's go with the flow. See what happens. This is how you sell something for the highest price, kiddos. You get the customer to name the price first."

"How do we do that?" Everett asked. They all stood in a circle on the street in front of the Wattersons' house. "Aren't they going to ask how much?"

"Maybe," DG said. "But we have a comeback. We say, 'How much do you think they're worth, ma'am?'"

"And what if they say 'Nothing'?" Linc said. He laughed, but no one else got the joke.

"Then we say, 'Do these puppies look worthless, ma'am?' 'No,' she'll say, and maybe she'll add, 'I can't offer you much.' Then we say, 'It's to support an important cause.' That's when we bring Jesse and Boop forward. We play on the customer's sympathies. We tell how Jesse and Boop need the money for stuff at home. That always gets them."

"But that would be lying, DG," Tina suddenly wailed. "I think we should just say, 'Five dollars or best offer.'"

"It's not lying," DG said. "Jesse does need it for house stuff. Better yet, it could be for his education. That always gets grownups."

"DG," Everett said. "Jesse wants to use the money to pay off Harley."

"No way we're doing it for that," DG said.

"But I have to pay him off," Jesse said. "That's the whole reason for this."

"Then it's a pretty poor reason," DG said, hardening his voice. "We're gonna take care of Harley. Look, what is this money for, really? What are you going to use it for, Jesse?"

Everyone turned to the black boy and waited. Jesse crinkled his brow. He finally said, "I don't know. All I was thinkin' was how to get Harley off my back."

Boop tugged at Jesse's shirtsleeve. "How about Mama and her operation, Jesse?" she said. "That's a good cause."

Jesse pursed his lips, then nodded. "Could be."

"What's that?" DG asked.

"My mom has bad kidneys. She has to be on a machine."

"For dialysis," DG said.

"Right," Jesse answered. "It's called a dialysis machine." He regarded DG with astonishment. "You are smart," he said. "Anyway, my mom's kidneys failed a while ago. So now she's lookin' for a transplant. When they find a donor, they gonna put one into her. She feels bad a lotta the time, though."

"Well, that does it!" DG said. "We have a 'Puppy-Thon' here. We're gonna sell these puppies to people who want to help Jesse's mother get her kidney! All the money's going to charity!"

"Do you think people will believe us?" Tina asked.

"Course they will!" DG answered, picking up a puppy. He fluffed its brown and black hair. "These guys are going to buy a lady a kidney! I bet people will really give for that! In fact, we can't just sell these dogs now—we'll have to auction them off to the highest bidder!"

"What are you talking about, DG?" Tina asked, stamping her foot. "We were just going to go up and down the street."

"This is much bigger than I thought!" DG said. "We can

really help someone out here. And give the dogs good homes too. Before we were just going to walk around and see who we could foist them off on. But now we have a cause."

Suddenly Everett caught the mood. "Yeah, I bet our Kairo group would help too. We could get kids to auction off other stuff at a big rally. Really make some money to help Jesse's mom."

"I don't know whether my mom would like that too much," Jesse said. "And what about Harley? He's gonna have my behind if I don't get him the money."

"I keep telling you, we're going to take care of Harley," DG said.

"But how? I ain't heard no 'hows' yet," Jesse said. His face had darkened with anger, and Everett could see that DG, as usual, was far out ahead of everyone.

"We'll work it out," DG said. "First, let's see how we can put on this campaign."

"I think," Everett interjected, "we'd better talk to Jesse's mom about it first."

"And our moms and dads," Tina said. "They're not going to want us involved in something this big without their permission."

"Okay, okay!" DG said. "Let's talk to our parents first. Then we talk to Everett's Kairo group. By the way, did Everett invite you guys?"

Everett felt the red rush up his neck and face when the others said no.

"What's a Kairo group?"

Everett started to explain, but DG said, "It's great. Lots of fun. You're all coming. This Friday, right, Ev?"

"Yeah, I guess." Everett was so stunned, he didn't know what else to say.

"Okay," DG said. "So now we have us, and the Kairo people, and the dogs at an auction. What else is there?"

"Harley," Jesse said unhappily.

"You keep coming back to that," DG said. "What are you worried about?"

"Harley's a mean dude," Jesse said. "I don't want me or Boop or my mom getting hurt."

"All right, what do you need?" DG asked.

"Ten dollars. He wants ten dollars from me every week. I was stealin' it from my mom, but then I felt bad about that. Now I don't know where to get it. I thought I'd sell the pups, that's all."

"All right, let's take an offering for this week," DG said.

"A what?" said the others.

DG laughed. "Isn't that what they do in church—take offerings for people in need?" He looked around at everyone, raising his eyebrows dramatically. "That is what they do, isn't it?"

"Yeah, but I don't have ten dollars," Linc said.

"How much you have?" DG asked.

"Two and change," Linc said.

"What about you?" DG looked at Everett, the Jewish boy's eyes piercing him like swords.

Everett thought for a second. "I think I have about four dollars and change. But I was saving it."

"This is more important," DG said with finality. "Tina, what about you?"

"A couple of dollars, I suppose."

"All right, and I have several dollars. So if Linc and Tina each give two, Everett gives three, and I give three, that adds up to ten."

"I don't expect you guys to give me the money," Jesse protested.

But Everett liked the idea. It would be the first time in his life he'd ever given money to someone he knew. Always before it was to the nameless "church" in a plate. But this was real. He forgot about the cost and the model he wanted to buy and said, "But that's just it. This is what we're supposed to do for one another. This is what they teach us at Kairo."

"They teach that?" Jesse asked.

"Yes, and more," DG said with such confidence that Everett blinked.

DG had never even been to a meeting yet! How did he know? But Everett just smiled. It was pure DG, that was for sure. Why not go with it?

"All right, let's get the money," DG said. "And even if it's going for something bad like Harley, we'll get it back somehow. So let's go for it. Here we started out to sell puppies, and now we have an auction and a cause. This is great."

"So we're not gonna try to sell them now?" Tina said.

"No," DG answered. "This is much bigger than we thought. Jesse, you should have told us about your mom before."

"I didn't think of it," Jesse said, shrugging.

"All right," DG said. "Everyone go home and get your money. Meet back here in ten minutes. Jesse, you and Boop can wait here and watch the dogs, or you can go with Linc and Tina."

"Okay," Jesse said, his eyes wide with wonder.

"Put your hands in!" DG exclaimed. Everyone formed a circle and put their hands in.

"For God, country, and Jesse's mom!" DG said. "Break!"

Everyone broke and Everett ran for his house, excited.

10
Thurston Farmer

Half an hour later, everyone was back. DG was full of ideas, and what he came up with sparked Everett, then Linc and Tina, and finally Jesse and Boop.

After a round of ideas, DG clapped his hands together. "We'll make posters and stuff and have a big rally. We'll plaster it all over the place."

"Yeah, and we could have a speaker, too!" Everett cried. Everyone turned to him.

"A speaker?" they said in unison.

"Yeah, they do it all the time at church. It's what brings in all the people. If we get someone who's famous and everyone knows about, then people come. They all get excited about seeing this person come in. It's great."

"But who could we get?" DG said. "And on such short notice?"

"Thurston Farmer!" Jesse said, and Boop clapped her hands this time.

"Even I know about him!" she said.

"The 76ers forward?" DG said.

"Yeah," Jesse said. "He does some projects in Philadelphia, I hear. Why not in New Castleton?"

"But he's really famous," Everett said. "Could we get him?"

"We can try!" DG said. "We'll have to find out how to write to him and tell him what it's all about. You can get your Kairo group to pray that he'll come," DG added. "I bet that would really get some things going if all those kids started praying."

"Yeah, I'm sure I can," Everett said. "Would you all like to talk to our youth pastor and tell him about this? I think it would work a lot better than just having me explain."

"Sure," DG said at once.

"It's a good plan," Jesse said. "We need a group behind it."

"Okay, I'll call him," Everett said. "Tonight."

"What can we do now?" DG asked.

"We can start designing the posters," Tina said. "I bet my dad would make copies at the office."

"And then we can start putting them up," Linc answered.

"But first we have to know if Thurston Farmer can come," Jesse said. "If he can come, that changes everything."

"Let's go write the letter now!" DG said. "We'll call the 76ers office and get the address. Let's go!"

They all filed into Linc and Tina's house. Everyone introduced Jesse and Boop to Mrs. Watterson, and she agreed to let the dog and puppies in.

When they told her about their grand plan, Mrs. Watterson just shook her head. "Whatever you want to do, I guess." She didn't quite seem to understand what was going on, but the kids didn't mind. They had work to do.

DG called the 76ers and got the address. Then they all stood around the typewriter as Tina typed out the letter.

Dear Mr. Farmer:

We are all fans of yours. We like to watch you play a lot, especially Jesse. But we also have a problem. Jesse's mom's kidneys do not work. She has to go on a dialysis machine a couple times a week and it is very hard. She is hoping to have a transplant. But to do that someone has to give a kidney, and it also takes a lot of money.

We think that if we had a big rally, we could get the money by donations. And if you came to the rally and spoke at it, it would even be better. That way, a lot of people will want to come. Also, Jesse's dog Queenie has four puppies and we want to auction off three to the highest bidders. (Boop gets the littlest one. She has named him Michael, not after anyone in particular, she just likes the name).

    If you can come to this, it would really be great. We think Jesse's mom would get a lot of hope from it. What do you think? We're planning to have the rally in the middle of September. That's way before basketball season, too, so maybe it'll be easier for you to fit it into your schedule. We know you're very famous and important, and if you can't come, we understand. But we really hope you can.

    Sincerely,

        The Kidney for Mrs. Hawkins Committee
            Jesse and Boop Hawkins
            Linc and Tina Watterson
                    DG Frankl
                  Everett Abels

    P.S. We'll still watch you play basketball, even if you can't come. But if you can come, we'll root all the more.

"It's great!" DG said when Tina typed in the last word. "He has to come."

"I think we'd better ask my mom before we mail it, though," Jesse said. "Just to make sure she's all right on this."

"Then let's go!" DG said. Everett hadn't seen him this excited in about a week!

Tina typed out the address on the envelope and put a

stamp on it, donated by Mrs. Watterson.

Then they made the trip back to the apartment complex. They were all excited as they walked up the path toward the complex between the two end buildings. Everyone talked enthusiastically about all they were going to do. It seemed like a party . . . until they crossed over into the main part of the complex.

There were Harley and his friends, coming right toward them.

11
Another Face-off

"Y o! Jesse! You in big trouble!" Harley swaggered down toward them. "Dint I tell you keep these whities out of here?" He walked right up to Jesse and grabbed him at the collar. "You got that ten?"

"Let him go!" DG yelled. "He has it!"

Harley's face curled into a sly smile. "Oh, you got it now, huh? Well let's see it." He let Jesse go.

Jesse took the ten dollar bills that Everett and the others had given him. Already he looked beaten, the excitement of the last few minutes drained away. Queenie growled at the bigger boy, baring black gums.

"Get this dog outa here!" Harley said, stepping back. "I

kill that dog I see it again."

Queenie suddenly lunged forward and snapped at Harley. Jesse jerked her back on the rope leash. "Queenie! Hush!"

Harley fell back into his little fivesome. "He ain't goin' hurt you, Harley!" one of them said.

"I don't like dogs!" Harley growled as he regained his balance. He counted the ten ones.

"All right," he said when he was finished. "You whities come around here again, gonna cost you. Else you get hurt. Bad."

DG's face steeled into a mask of anger. Everett grabbed him at his arm before he could take a swing at Harley.

"Oh, you wanta fight?" Harley said, jumping forward and jabbing the air in front of DG.

Queenie leaped. She got hold of Harley's wrist and bit!

Harley screamed, jerking his hand out of her mouth.

There was confusion for a moment, then Jesse pulled Queenie back.

Harley backed up. "I tell you, I'm gonna kill that dog." He cursed and shook his hand. There was a little blood at the tooth marks. Queenie had really bitten him.

"Come on, Harley," one of the others said. "Let's go. We got the money."

Backing up, Harley seethed, "I'm gonna get you, Jesse. Ten more next week. And all you whities—ten for each of you. Or we strike."

"We'll sic Queenie on you!" DG yelled.

"That dog gonna die, man!" Harley screamed back. Then his friends pulled him away, and they all went off up the street. Harley shook his hand with pain.

DG patted Queenie while Jesse loosened her rope. "Looks like you have a secret weapon," DG said. "Queenie seems to know Harley's an enemy."

"He kicked her a couple of times about six months ago," Jesse said. "She's hated him ever since. He's not a nice guy."

"Let's get to your house and talk to your mom," Everett said. "I think we need to get out of here as soon as possible. I don't have another ten dollars."

"Neither do any of us," Linc said. He jabbed the air, imagining his fist connecting with Harley's face. "I think he's a coward. If he doesn't have his four sidekicks with him, he's nothing."

"You right about that," Jesse said. He led them down the sidewalk. They turned up the little sidewalk to the apartment on the main floor. A moment later they were inside.

Mrs. Hawkins was pleasant and friendly. She sat them all down in the living room. The furniture—a pink velour sofa, two easy chairs, and a table or two, all of it nicked and in bad condition—was quickly filled up.

Jesse introduced all the kids around. "These are my new friends, Mom." He didn't tell her about the money, but Everett was sure he didn't tell her things like that. She probably wouldn't want to know.

She was still wearing the blue robe and smoking a

cigarette. Jesse told her about the plan.

"I don't expect no charity on this," Mrs. Hawkins said.

DG jumped in. "It's not charity. It's what friends do for friends. We want to help. And you're not going to be able to do it on your own."

"That's true," she said, stubbing out the cigarette. "You kids all want a drink? I have Cokes and ginger ales."

Soon everyone was sipping a fresh drink. Mrs. Hawkins looked tired and worn out. Jesse said the dialysis had been done two days before, and on the third day she was at her worst.

Mrs. Hawkins agreed. "It's wearing me down, that's for sure."

When Jesse told her about Thurston Farmer, Mrs. Hawkins whistled. "Now that would be somethin', him comin' out here. I would love to see that."

"We already made up the letter to him," Jesse explained. "So if you're willin' to go with it, we want to do it."

"I'm not gonna stop you," she said finally, lighting another cigarette.

Normally, DG was very much against smoking, and Everett was glad he didn't say anything.

Mrs. Hawkins finished by saying, "I guess if you're gonna sell those pups for my operation, I should let them stay here."

"I was hoping you'd say that, Mom," Jesse said. He took Queenie and the pups back into his room. Leading the other kids back there, Boop showed them a big poster of

Thurston Farmer.

"Jesse got it last Christmas," Boop said.

The kids all went back outside, leaving the pups in Jesse's room. Queenie came with them, still on the rope leash. Jesse said, "I feel safer with her. She's not afraid of Harley the way I am."

"Let's mail the letter," Tina said. She was still holding it. "And then let's get planning the rest of this thing. If it's gonna be in three weeks, we don't have much time."

"I know," Everett suddenly said, feeling kind of left out of things for the moment. "Let's go to the tree fort. We can make Jesse and Boop honorary members."

"Good idea!" DG said. "We haven't been there in a few days."

12
Story

An hour later, they were all sitting on the first floor of the tree fort. Queenie lay on the ground underneath. Jesse had taken off her leash once they were out of the complex and away from people. "She minds me normally," he said, "so I don't need to tie her up."

They all told stories, shared cupcakes, and laughed together. DG had Jesse carve his initials in the fort. Then Boop tried to do hers, but Tina ended up finishing it for her. DG showed Jesse and Boop the "defensive capability" of the tree fort. He demonstrated the net that fell down over any intruders. They all showed off their slingshot ability. DG even set up a target and everyone hit it at least once, except Boop who didn't want to try. She was sure she'd whirl it around and hit herself in the face.

After the fun, though, everyone sat around talking about Harley. "What are we going to do about that guy he met with?" Tina said. "It seems like that's a bigger problem than anything else."

They all moved into a circle, sitting cross-legged.

"Why can't we go to the police?" Tina asked. She looked around at everyone, waiting for an answer, but no one said anything right away.

Finally Boop said, "Ever-time the police come in, little kids get hurt. No one talks about it, but it's so."

"What happens?" DG asked Jesse.

"If the police nail one of the big guys, then all the smaller guys go out and hurt the kids. They just get mean to them. It gets dirty. There's too many of them for the police to stop."

"But Harley's only got four others in his gang," Everett commented.

"Harley's part of a bigger gang," Jesse said. "It all goes with turf. Either you join, you buy protection, or you get hurt. Or shot, like that kid a couple weeks ago."

"What happened with that?" Everett asked.

"No one's found out," Jesse said. "He was shot at night on the street. No one's talking. The police got no clues. But he was one of the ones who wouldn't pay."

"Then why don't kids tell the police?" Tina wailed.

"That's the best thing to do."

"Not if the police can't protect you all the time," Jesse said. "That's twenty-four hours a day. You go with who's got the power. The police only got the power when they're around. The moment they're not, everyone's in danger."

There was a sudden crack behind them. Into the clearing stepped Seth Williamson and his two Dobermans, Whip and Bump.

"Hi, Seth," the kids said, and they all hopped down to the ground. Queenie growled, but when Whip and Bump loped over and gave her a friendly sniff, everyone seemed okay.

Seth was an old construction worker who lived on the other side of the woods from Linc and Tina and Everett. He looked grizzled, wore hunting gear, and told great stories. The kids often went to him for advice.

"Hi, kids. Been wondering what you were up to."

DG introduced Jesse and Boop. "They live down the creek," DG said. "We met them when we paddled there in Linc and Tina's boats." He explained about their little expedition.

"You guys are real pioneers," Seth said. He wore his farmer overalls and a green hat that said John Deere on it. Everyone sat back down, and Seth joined them. "So what are you doin'—tellin' stories?" he asked.

"Do you have a story for us?" Everett said, always one to ask. He liked Seth's stories, especially the way he dramatized them.

"How about one to go along with Jesse's problem?" DG said, as Seth smiled and scratched his grizzled face.

"So what is Jesse's problem?" Seth asked.

Everyone turned to Jesse and then to DG to explain. DG took the lead. He laid it all out in a few minutes, while Seth rubbed his beard and nodded as he listened.

When DG was finished, Seth said, "Sounds serious. But you know what the policeman said about your problem with Chuck Davis last month. You should go to the police. Get them involved."

Jesse shook his head and told Seth what he had told the others before. "Something has to happen to change the whole community's attitude. Everyone has to get in on it and support it, or it don't work. And most of the people don't seem to care. Least that's the way it looks to me."

DG told Seth about the rally they were planning. "Maybe that would be the thing," he said. "If we can get Thurston Farmer to come, it could really do something."

Seth nodded. "Thurston's a Christian, too. He could be counted on to give a gospel message, if you asked him."

"I didn't know that," Everett said.

"He's not real vocal about it," Seth said. "But I heard him speak once in my church. He's a real committed man."

"But he's not going to convert the whole community," DG said. He had a slightly sour look on his face that Everett didn't like. Was DG turning off to the idea now that he knew Thurston was a Christian? He hoped not.

"Well, let me tell you about someone in the Bible," Seth

said. "Jesus was comin' down the street one day with all his disciples. And he had got real famous by then. Healing the sick. Raising the dead. Cleansing lepers. Feeding the five thousand. People were lined up to see him. They all wanted something."

"It sounds like a parade," Boop said.

"That's right, girl, it was," Seth said, reaching out and tousling her hair. "It was a regular Fourth of July let-it-all-hang-out national celebration! They were hangin' from the trees! In fact, there was one guy, this little guy, no more than four-and-a-half feet tall."

"A midget?" Linc asked.

"No, just short stuff, that's all. His name was—"

"Zaccheus!" Everett cried, throwing his arms up.

"You got it," Seth said. "You kids know the song?"

"What song?" DG asked.

Everett sang, "Zaccheus was a wee little man, a wee little man was he!"

"That's right," Seth said. "He was a wee little man, and he couldn't see a thing in the parade. Everyone towered over him. But since he was so small, he'd learned somethin' early on: how to climb trees. Little guys are usually great tree climbers, right, Everett?"

Everyone knew what a great tree climber Everett was, even though he wasn't so small. He was taller than DG anyway, though not as tall as Linc. "Right," Everett said.

"So Zaccheus is walkin' around. He's lookin' for a tree, a tree he can slide up so he can see the goings on. He doesn't want to stand out or anything, he just wants to see what's happenin' in town today. So he finds this old sycamore tree. Lots of low branches. A little sappy and slick, but perfect for his purposes. And he starts up." Seth pretended he was climbing, and he grunted here and there to make it sound more dramatic.

"He climbs up high, high above all the heads. And some of the people notice him up there and they laugh. 'There's little old Zaccheus,' they're sayin'. 'Best tree climber in Israel!' And they slap their knees and laugh. 'Who you lookin' for, Zaccheus—the man in the moon?' And, 'What if that branch breaks and you fall right on top of Jesus, what you gonna do then, little Zaccheus?' Well, that little man didn't say a thing. He just wanted to see. So he smiled. And anyway, a lot of people didn't like Zaccheus too much. You know why?"

" 'Cause he was a criminal?" Jesse asked.

"Almost!" Seth said. "He was a tax collector!"

"That's not so bad," DG said. "Unless you're an adult."

"Then it's real bad," Tina added, and everyone laughed. "My dad hates paying taxes."

"So did everyone back then," Seth said. "And when some of them saw Zaccheus climb that tree, they were ready to throw a tomato or two. 'Who you think you are, little man?' 'Get down from there, tax collector, and act like the rest of us!'

"Zaccheus ignored them all. He was used to being powerful and he wasn't about to give in to their taunts. So he's lookin' down the street, and along comes Jesus with his whole group following him. They're just sashayin' along, having a great time. The people are shoutin' and yellin' and hurrahin,' and Jesus is just lopin' along like he has all the time in the world. If it was today, he'd be signin' autographs. But he was stoppin' and givin' a little baby a kiss and a toddler a pat on the head. And sayin' to one of the ladies he's glad she made it and that things are gonna work out in her family. Stuff like that. Everyone's real happy. Except one person."

"Zaccheus!" everyone shouted.

"No!" Seth said. "Jesus!"

"Jesus?" everyone answered. "He's the center of attention."

"But he's got more on his mind than pleasin' a crowd. Jesus wants to help fix up a town problem. So he walks along and then suddenly he's right under Zaccheus's limb. The little tax collector is hanging out there right in the road. Not more'n five feet from Jesus' nose! And guess what everyone's thinkin'?"

"That Zaccheus will fall off?" DG said, and everyone laughed.

"No!" Seth said. "That Jesus will tell Zaccheus off. For being such a rotten person as to collect taxes for Rome from the people of Israel! But Jesus fools them all. He looks up at that little man and he says, 'Come on down, Zaccheus!' "

"That's what they say on TV," Jesse said, laughing. "Come on down—to Florida or somethin.' "

"Right," Seth said. "Well, this is Jericho, I think, and Zaccheus is the chief tax collector there, and everyone crowds around. They figure Jesus is really goin' to lay something on the little guy. Tell him off. Teach him a thing or two. But you know what Jesus says? He says, 'Zaccheus, come down, because you and I are going to eat dinner together.'

"And everyone is outraged! Jesus is gonna eat with the worst guy in the whole town? He's gonna be friends with him? Zaccheus hurries up and climbs down. Nothin' like this ever happened to him before. Before, all the people crossed over to the other side of the street when he went by. But now a famous teacher is gonna dine with him!"

"So Jesus approved of him?" DG said. "Is Jesus for taxes or something?"

"No, DG," Seth said. "In fact, as Jesus and Zaccheus walked along, Jesus talked to him about his tax thing. And suddenly Zaccheus stopped the whole crowd and said anyone he'd overcharged, he'd pay them back four times whatever he owed them! The whole place went berserk! That was a lot of money, because Zaccheus must have overcharged every one of them a time or two.

"It's an amazing story," Seth continued, "because no one ever treated a tax collector decent before. And none of them ever repented for cheating the people before. But both things happened that day. That's the effect Jesus has on people."

"And what our rally could do," DG said.

"If we can bring it off," Jesse added.

"You never know what the Lord can do when He gets involved," Seth said, patting his knees and standing up. "I got to be movin' along now. I see my doggies and yours are gettin' along fine now." Seth pointed to the three dogs romping in the open area in front of the tree fort. Queenie and Whip were having a tug of war over a stick.

"Thanks for coming by, Seth," Everett said. Everyone walked him to the edge of the tree fort area.

"I just wanted to check on you," he said. "Glad I caught you down here. I'll be prayin' about your rally there."

When he was gone, DG said, "I hope our rally has an effect, but I don't think Thurston Farmer is Jesus."

Everett was thinking hard about the story, though. Something in it clicked with him, something that was important, but he wasn't sure what it was. He'd have to keep thinking about it.

13
Explanations

Everett, DG, Linc, and Tina all sat in Everett's living room with Jeff Simmons, the youth pastor from Everett's church.

"It sounds like a great idea," Jeff said. "But I'm not sure we can get Thurston Farmer to come."

"Leave that to us," DG said. "We already sent the letter. I guarantee it. He'll come."

No one had told Jeff about Harley, though, or the drug deal. Everett couldn't decide whether to tell him or not. He thought being completely honest was wiser. But would that kill the whole thing?

"I admire your enthusiasm and confidence," Jeff said to DG. "But Farmer's a pretty important dude."

"Not too important to help some needy people," DG countered.

"Well, look," Jeff said. "We'll have the rally at the church—"

"No way!" DG interrupted. "We can't have it at a church. Too many people won't feel good about coming."

"Then where?" Jeff said. He looked uneasy.

"Right in the park in front of Jesse's apartments," DG said. "Isn't that where we should have it?" He looked at Everett, Linc, and Tina. "By the way, why isn't Jesse here?"

"He's supposed to be," Everett said. "But he just didn't show. I agree—I think we should have it in the park."

"Lot of church people won't want to come down there," Jeff answered.

"Then what good is it?" DG said. "If we can't get the churches to agree on this, what good is it?"

"Oh, now we're getting other churches involved?" Jeff asked.

"All of them in the area," DG said. "And the synagogue, too. This is a community thing!"

"All right, all right," Jeff replied. "And we're going to do all this in three weeks?"

"Right after the start of school," DG said. "The sooner we deal with Harley, the better."

Everett winced. Now that let it all out.

Jeff pounced. "Who's Harley?"

DG glanced around at the others, obviously realizing that he'd said what he shouldn't have. But Everett just sighed. He felt better letting Jeff know everything. Everett explained to the youth pastor about Harley, the drug situation, and everything else.

Jeff was strangely quiet during the whole talk. When Everett finished, he said, "Kids, this is really dangerous. These people are playing for keeps. Do you know what you're getting into?"

"We have to help Jesse and his mom, that's all," DG said. "And we think it might have an effect on the neighborhood, too. Clean it up some."

Everett broke in, "We're hoping Harley and his friends will realize the bad in what they're doing."

Jeff rubbed his chin skeptically. "I don't know. This is going to be rough. What if Harley and his friends realize what you're up to, and decide to disturb the whole rally?"

"I know," Everett answered. "I was thinking about that too."

"Yeah," DG admitted. "It's a possibility. But we just have to hope for the best. What else can we do? Harley will do whatever he wants no matter what we say. So we'll just have to try to give him good reason to change."

"All right," Jeff said. "But I think we should talk to the police, too. They'll have to be involved to keep the crowd under control. We don't need a possible riot on our hands."

There was a knock at the door, and Everett went to answer. When he opened it, there stood Jesse and Boop.

Jesse's face was covered with blood.

"What happened?" Everett cried.

Everyone ran to the door as Jesse stumbled in. "Harley punched me in the face," he said. "Made my nose bleed."

Mrs. Abels led Jesse to the kitchen where she washed him up.

"Harley just hauled off and socked him," Boop said. "For nothin.' Really for nothin.' "

Jesse shook his head. "It wasn't for nothin,' Boop. I was sneakin' around trying to catch Harley in a drug deal. I had a little camera, and he saw me and broke the camera."

"But you didn't take any pictures," Boop said.

"I was trying to," Jesse said to Everett. "I'm sorry I'm late. Is the meeting over?"

Mrs. Abels pronounced Jesse all right. "It's just a bloody nose," she said. "Nothing broken, or you'd really hurt."

Everyone went back into the living room, and Mrs. Abels brought in some cookies and milk. After setting them down, she said, "Jeff, I know everyone here is excited about this project, but from what I've just seen, I don't know that I want Everett involved in it."

"Mommmm!" Everett cried.

"Don't mom me!" Mrs. Abels said. "Look at your friend Jesse. He could have had his nose broken. There are bad people over there, and I want you to be very careful what you do in this. All of you. It's dangerous. I know how much you want to help, but sometimes interfering creates more problems than it solves. There, I've said it. Now you're all going to have to convince me that no one will be hurt anymore."

Everyone was silent for a moment, then Jeff said, "I think the kids have a good idea, Mrs. Abels. The execution of it has to be fine-tuned. But we'll be okay. We'll stick together in groups, and there will be adults with them at all times. I guarantee that."

"Well, do what you think is best, Jeff," Mrs. Abels said. "But I want all the parents involved in this from the beginning."

"You've got it." Jeff turned to the group as Mrs. Abels went out of the room.

Everett felt as though he should apologize, though he wasn't sure for what. "She's just trying to make sure no one gets hurt," he said.

Jeff said, "This kind of thing takes careful planning, gang. You haven't given yourselves much time. But I'll help as much as I can. Let's get out some preliminary flyers, let people know. We don't have to mention Thurston Farmer yet. We can put up some posters, and I'll talk to the other churches. Let's tell Kairo about this on Friday and get as many kids involved as we can. I'll see about getting some adults involved. And the other thing we should do is to get some kind of Christian band."

"A rap band!" Jesse said right away, smiling.

DG frowned, but then he smiled. "I guess I shouldn't expect this to be a Bar Mitzvah type singalong!"

Everyone laughed, but Jesse said, "There are a lot of rap

bands around, but I don't know about Christian. How do we find 'em?"

"What if we make it a whole battle of the bands?" DG said suddenly. "What if we invite all of them and give out trophies to the winners or something?"

"Now there's an idea," Jeff said. "That will really bring out the people. Even older folks might want to see that."

"Boy, three weeks," DG said. "Seems like we don't have enough time now."

"We'll do it," Jeff said. "I know a local Christian DJ who would get the word out. And you can go put up posters that will get the bands to sign up to play. That ought to bring them in."

By the end of the week, Linc and Tina had a poster ready. It read:

BATTLE OF THE BANDS
Christian Rap Group Rally September 14th
Rap Groups Sign Up to Play
Call: 555-3140
Raise Money to help Mrs. Hawkins get her kidney!
Special Speaker Yet to be Announced but He will be Famous!
Queenie's Puppies Auctioned Off
Come one, come all!
No admission. The plate will be passed.

Jeff and the group went into the community and put up the posters. Churches were called and several indicated interest in being a part. Everett called up the local newspaper and got a story in about how they were all praying that Thurston Farmer would come and speak. Several Christian rap group leaders called and said they wanted to be included. Jeff found a church that had some powerful audio equipment, and they volunteered to run the sound. By Friday they had chairs lined up and adults who would set them out. The police agreed to send over several cars for crowd control.

Then Jesse's mom went into the hospital with a serious infection. Jesse said this happened a lot.

"We've got to move fast!" DG said to everyone.

That night, Everett and DG spoke to the Kairo group. All the kids immediately liked the idea. Parents and kids volunteered to put up posters everywhere they could. Soon the whole town of New Castleton was plastered with news of the rally. It sounded like five thousand people would be there!

But no one had heard from Thurston Farmer.

"I say we call him on the phone," DG said. "See if he got our letter." He, Linc and Tina, Everett, and Jesse and Boop were all sitting around Linc and Tina's pool trying to decide what to do. Everything was going so well, but Thurston Farmer hadn't made a peep.

"But we don't have his number," Everett answered. "And the 76ers office won't give it to us. I already tried."

"We have to do something!" DG said.

"I have an idea," Tina said quietly. "Linc and I were

talking about it. You know how Channel 2 always has local things on the news? Why don't we get on Channel 2?"

"How do you do that?" Jesse asked.

It was a clear, hot day. Everyone had already had a dip in the pool. They had fought some boat battles, too. Now the kids sat on the side of the pool, dangling their legs in the water.

"Everett got us into the newspaper once already," Tina said. "How did you do that?"

"I just called, and a reporter came over my house," Everett answered. "It was simple."

"Let's do it!" DG announced. "Let's go for it."

That afternoon a TV truck came around, and that night the six kids were all on TV. The reporter mentioned that they were all praying Thurston Farmer would come. At the end, the reporter said, "Thurston Farmer, if you're listening, you can answer these kids' prayers."

Even Jesse's mom saw the news clip from her hospital bed. She called and told Jesse, "All the nurses were gathered around cheering me on."

But there was still no call from Thurston Farmer.

14
The Philidelphia Spectrum

"Well, where does he practice basketball?" DG said as the six of them sat glumly out by the pool again.

"Probably the Philadelphia Spectrum," Jesse answered. "That's where the 76ers play."

"Then let's go over there and try to find him," DG said. "He couldn't resist a face-to-face confrontation. We'll do him in with charm."

"How do we get there?" Everett asked. They couldn't walk all the way into Philadelphia.

"What about Jeff Simmons?" DG said. "He can drive."

"Great idea," Linc said. "Can you call him, Evvie?"

In five minutes it was arranged. The kids called their parents, and they all gave their permission. Jeff drove them to the Spectrum. It was situated on a huge city corner and took up a whole block. In fact, with parking it was several blocks. Everett had never been to the Spectrum before, but DG had. They all walked right up to the ticket office.

Jeff stepped up to the window. "We'd like to get in to see a practice," he said.

"Sorry, the Spectrum isn't open right now," the attendant said. "If you want tickets for a game, I can sell them to you."

"But can't we just get in to speak to someone?"

"I'm sorry. The Spectrum is closed."

They walked away, feeling deflated. DG, though, was still determined. "Look," he said, "we knew this was going to happen. Now we go into Plan B."

"What's that?" Jeff asked. He still wasn't used to DG's brainstorms.

"Let's look for the garbage exit."

They walked around the building till they found a truck entrance. There were large dumpsters in the area, but the doors were locked. There was a buzzer next to the door.

"Okay, this is what we do," DG said. He explained his plan. Jeff wasn't sure it was honest, but everyone said it was the only way. Finally Jeff agreed, to Everett's relief.

DG, Everett, Jesse, Linc, Tina, and Boop hid behind one of the dumpsters. Jeff walked up to entrance door and pressed the buzzer. A few minutes later, someone answered.

Everett heard Jeff say to the man, "There's something out here you'd better take a look at."

The man was dressed in a blue janitorial uniform. Jeff led him back to the dumpsters and started pointing and gesturing while the six kids hurried to the open door and slid in.

"Home free," DG said.

"Not yet," Everett answered. "Now we have to find our way to the main floor."

They crept through the causeways, stopping, listening, and waiting till it looked clear. Soon they came out onto one of the main concession areas. There was no one about, but they could hear a basketball bouncing inside and men's voices.

They came around a corner. There stood a security guard.

"Hey, you kids, what are you going here?"

Everyone ran down past the empty concessions. The security guard shouted into a walkie-talkie, "Some kids in the building. Need back-up."

DG yelled, "Into the stands."

They all ran into the first entranceway they found. Coming out into the seats, they saw the basketball court. There were two teams playing in sweats. Someone blew a whistle. No one paid any attention to the kids. The security guard ran into the tunnel and came out above the kids. He talked into his walkie-talkie and yelled at the kids.

"You're not supposed to be here, you kids! Stay where you are."

"Out to the railings below!" DG yelled.

They jumped from seat to seat, keeping on the armrests. It was hard going, but soon they reached the lower railing. Everett looked behind him. Now there were three security guards.

Suddenly Jesse leaned out over the railing. "Thurston! Thurston Farmer!"

The basketball court suddenly echoed with an eerie silence. All ten of the players were looking up at the stands.

Jesse yelled, "We need your help, Thurston! Will you help us?"

Everett shouted, "We were the ones on the news! Did you see us?"

And DG said, "We want you to come to our rally!"

The three security guards cornered the kids. One stood above them in the seats. The other two came in on the sides.

"Please, Mr. Farmer!" Jesse cried.

Someone threw a ball to one of the players. As the security guards moved in, one of the players said, "Looks like it's up to you, Thurs. Those kids are caught."

Thurston Farmer walked to the edge of the court. "You're the kids who were on the news?"

One of the security guards grabbed Everett and DG. "We've got them, fellas. You can go back to your game."

"No!" Thurston Farmer said. He was an impressive sight—six-foot-six inches tall, and his head was bald. "Bring them all down to the court."

"What?" yelled the security guards.

"You heard me. Bring them down to the court. I want to talk to them."

The guard let go of Everett and DG. The kids all climbed back over the seats, and the three guards led them down to the main concourse. They came out onto the first floor. The basketball court loomed up before them. There stood ten of the biggest, strongest looking men any of the kids had ever seen.

"So you were the ones on TV?" Thurston Farmer said. The other players crowded around.

"We need you to come, Thurston," DG said. "Jesse's mom—" He turned to Jesse. "Well, maybe I better let Jesse do the talking."

Jesse introduced everyone. Then he went through the whole Philadelphia 76ers lineup. "This is Thurston. And that really giant man there is Grant Littlefield. And this is Jimmy Wallace." He named them all, just as if they were family.

Thurston Farmer boomed a loud, friendly laugh. "What do you say, boys? Should I assist these folks in their time of need?"

"Your call, Thurs," Jimmy Wallace said with a big grin.

"All right," Thurston Farmer said. "If you've all gone to all this trouble, how can I refuse? How did you get in here anyway?"

"By my door!" a man yelled behind them. Everyone turned around and there stood Jeff and the janitor.

Everyone laughed.

"You are smart kids," Thurston said. He flipped the ball to Jesse. "You play basketball?"

"Sure do!" Jesse said. He bounced the ball a couple of times and shot it back.

"Well, come on, let's go to it. A little one-on-six!"

Thurston led the kids out onto the court. He set the six of them up in position and said, "If you can steal the ball, it's yours!"

He then began bouncing the ball and started a drive. Weaving in and out among the kids, he soon had everyone shouting and cheering. Jeff stood on the sidelines, talking with the other players. In a moment, the ball whooshed through the hoop. Two points!

"Come on, kids!" Thurston said. "You can stop me!"

He bobbed, drove, wove, and moved. It was marvelous. Everett almost didn't want to play so he could stand back and watch the man do his moves. Then the other 76ers came out onto the court and threw the ball around. Jesse and DG tried to steal it, but could get nowhere.

"Hey," DG suddenly said, "why don't we choose up teams?" He raised his eyebrows dramatically.

Thurston grinned, and in a minute it was two teams of two 76ers and three kids each. They played for about fifteen minutes. Thurston even passed the ball to Everett, who took a shot and made it. The whole event was amazing. In the end, Thurston promised to come to the rally and speak. He gave Jeff his office number, and everything was settled.

On the way home, DG said, "I told you we could do it."
"I'll never doubt you again," Jeff said, and everyone
laughed.

15
Harley Snarley

What do you think you're doin'?"

The voice sounded hard and nasty. Everett, DG, and Jesse turned around. It was Harley. He was alone this time, but just as nasty as ever.

"We're putting up posters," Jesse answered. He bunched up his lower lip and looked ready for a fight.

Everett tightened his stomach, thinking if Harley hit him, a hard stomach would ward off the blow.

Harley ripped a poster out of DG's hand. "So you got some big-time basketball player to come, huh?"

"Thurston Farmer," Jesse said coolly. "He's the best."

"Not better than Michael Jordan or Charles Barkley."

"Just as good."

"Well, I'll tell you what," Harley said. "I'll just take all those posters myself. Maybe I'll put up some—in the men's toilet!"

He lunged forward, but DG pulled the sheaf of posters behind his back. Jesse danced forward.

"You want to fight, fight me," Jesse said, putting up his fists.

"I'll fight when I'm ready," Harley said, stepping back. He was about six inches taller than any of them and could probably take on all three of them at once.

Everett told himself to get ready.

"Guess I'll just have to rip down ever-one you put up," Harley said, striding to the telephone pole and ripping off the poster. "You think this is gonna turn anyone on? No way!"

He tore the poster into little bits. Then he blew the bits into Jesse's face. "You want somethin' that'll turn you on? You see me. I got plenty of stuff that'll turn you on."

"What, drugs?" Jesse said with a sneer.

"Maybe. Say, where's that ten dollars you owe me for this week?"

Jesse stepped back. He kept his eyes right on Harley. "I ain't payin' that no more!"

Harley suddenly leaped forward, clasping Jesse at the neck. DG flailed at him, but Harley just pushed him away. Harley was too big and strong. Everett started forward, but

Harley gave him a stern look, then popped him on the jaw. The punch stung, and Everett reeled back.

Harley still had Jesse by the throat.

"You don't mess with me, hear? I'll take you apart."

Jesse wheezed and tried to breathe. Obviously, his windpipe was cut off. DG grabbed Harley's arm and tried to break the hold. With his left hand, Harley knocked him away again. DG fell to the ground, the posters flying every which way. Then Harley turned to Everett. "You want a kick you know where? Then keep comin'!"

Everett froze. Then he leaped.

Harley got him right in the groin. Everett fell to the ground in pain.

DG tried to scramble up, but Harley gave him a hard kick to the thigh. DG rolled over in pain. Harley still had Jesse at the throat. "Now it's twenty dollars. Have it by tomorrow, or I'll mess up your sister. Hear?"

He let go of Jesse, and the boy slumped to the pavement. He coughed and choked. Then he began crying. "I don't have no twenty dollars, Harley. I have nothin.' My mom's in the hospital. I don't have no twenty."

"Then get it," Harley bristled. "Or I'm goin' after your sister." He turned and walked away, laughing.

Jesse sat on the ground crying while DG and Everett came up on either side of him and put their arms around him.

"It'll be okay," DG said. "We'll get twenty somehow."

Jesse shook his head. "Then it'll be thirty, and forty.

Soon it'll be a hundred. You can't do that much. I can't do that."

Everett said, "Jesse, how about if you and Boop come home with me? You can stay at my house until the rally. You know what they say in the movies—you get heat, you lie low. Stay out of sight. If Harley can't find you, he can't make you pay."

"That's a great idea!" DG said. "Why didn't I think of that?"

Jesse said, "Would your mom and dad let us do that?"

"I'll talk them into it. My mom saw your bloody nose. She knows your mom is in the hospital and all you have is your aunt taking care of you. So why not?"

"I just never thought . . ." Jesse said.

"What—that white people would help black people?" DG asked.

"Yeah," Jesse said. "I mean, I don't know too many white folks."

"Well, now you do," Everett said, trying to figure out how he would break this to his mom. Boop could sleep with his sister. That would work. And Jesse could sleep in the guest room. Why not?

DG and Everett put their arms under Jesse's armpits and lifted him up. "Come on. Let's find Boop," DG said. "And get Queenie and the puppies. We can hide them down at the tree fort if our moms won't let them come into the house. Deal?"

DG held up his fist, and Everett and Jesse punched it.

"Come on, let's get the rest of these posters up," DG said. "Even if Harley rips them down, we have to do what we can now while the sun is shining."

They continued up the street. The posters had a picture in black and white of Thurston Farmer leaping to slam-dunk the ball in the 76ers basket. It was a beautiful shot, and Thurston had even signed pictures for all the kids.

The kids worked down both sides of the street. They taped or stapled the posters to telephone poles, mailboxes, anything that stood upright. Harley didn't return, but they all kept a lookout.

When they got together at the end of the street, Jesse said, "I can't go around for the rest of my life bein' afraid of that guy."

"I know," DG said. "But there's a time to fight and a time to get ready to fight. A time to go and a time to flow. A time to ride the rails and a time to bide your time."

"Where did you get that?" Everett asked.

"The Bible—sort of," DG said. He winked. "My version."

Mrs. Abels agreed to let Boop and Jesse stay at the house for a few days until things calmed down. Meanwhile, the kids kept putting up posters. People from the Kairo group helped in other communities. The kids invited people from all over, including Seth Williamson and Mr. Hennessee. Whenever they went down the creek to Jesse's house, they stopped and played with the dogs for a while.

They had all became good friends with Duke, Charlie, and the other twenty-five. Jesse brought up Queenie and let her play with them too.

Meanwhile, the sound system was put together. Various bands signed up to be included. By the end of the next week, they had five bands who wanted to compete, including one made up entirely of junior high kids.

Several churches had agreed to participate. They also posted notices in their bulletins. DG set up a "hotline" at his house with an answering machine that gave out information.

Coming up to the last week before the rally, Jesse had avoided Harley all week. The next week, though, school started. He and Boop would have to return to their apartment. Jesse told Everett he was worried about going back. What would Harley do?

The Friday before the big event, DG, Everett, and Jesse heard voices in the woods as they were walking to Jesse's house. They crept back to where the voices were. In a moment, they all saw what it was: Harley having another meeting with the drug man. Same clearing. Same place. DG motioned to them all to creep up to the stump and hide.

At the stump, they all squeezed behind and listened. Harley and the man were talking about different kids who were problems in the community.

"They don't want to buy," Harley said.

"Well, make them buy," the man said. "Take them out in woods and make them try it. That's the way you do it, boy. Get them hooked. I'll meet you here tomorrow night with the stuff. You better pull it off, boy."

"I will. But you want to meet during the rally?"

"Sure, best time. That rally is nothin', man. You're not goin' to it, are you?"

Harley shuffled his feet nervously. "I was plannin' to do some messin' around, yeah."

"Well, we got bigger fish to fry."

DG climbed up the dangling roots on the back of the trunk. Jesse and Everett peeked out on either side. Harley and his four thug-buddies stood in a semicircle about the man.

"I wish we had a camera," DG whispered. He hung high above them on the sideways stump, his feet resting on the roots. Everett's heart banged in his chest. They should just get away now, he was sure of that. Something bad would happen if they didn't.

And then it did.

DG slipped and a root cracked.

Immediately, Harley and the others turned. "What was that?"

"Over there!"

DG jumped down from the stump. "Run!" he shrieked.

Everett and Jesse popped up and ran. DG was out ahead. Harley and the four others were behind, still trying to see what it was.

DG got out to the creek and started for the complex, but two of Harley's friends had already cut them off.

"To the trail!" DG cried.

The three boys ran up the trail. Soon Everett was out of breath and drawing hard. His lungs burned.

Up ahead of them the overpass loomed. Harley and the others were gaining on the trail behind them, about a hundred yards back.

Soon they reached the concrete under the overpass.

"Into the tunnel," Jesse yelled. "I know a way."

They all ran into the tunnel. At first the light from the opening shone far enough so that they could see. But soon it was very dark, just a gray film of light barely seeping through. They all slowed to a walk.

"Keep in the middle," Jesse said. There was no water this time, because it hadn't rained. "Feel for the down part of the curve."

"I got it," Everett answered.

DG brought up the rear now. All three boys were huffing like the big bad wolf. Everett was tired already. "They have us cornered in here!" he said.

"Not if we can get out," Jesse said. "Keep on going."

At the end of the tunnel they heard voices. "Now we got you," Harley called. His voice echoed in the chamber. Everett could hear them stomping up behind them. He thought, *Jesse had better be right, because if he's wrong we are nailed!*

Above them there was a sudden shrieking of bats.

Everett held his hands over his head and flailed at the wings beating around him. In a moment, they all passed.

"Maybe the bats will scare them away," Jesse said. But he plowed on. Everett listened to the slap of his feet on the damp bottom of the culvert.

Behind them, lights flickered in the darkness.

"What is it?" Everett whispered.

"They have cigarette lighters," DG said.

Harley kept up a chatter as they walked. "I'm gonna get you this time. Leave all of you for dead!"

Everett plugged on, telling himself to stay calm. The culvert narrowed. He could feel the walls closing on either side. Jesse said, "It's only up a little ways."

"What is?" DG said.

"You'll see."

Everett couldn't see anything. But up ahead, he suddenly noticed a tiny spot of light. A hole in the ceiling!

A moment later, they stood under it. A little circle of light shone on the ceiling.

"What is it?" Everett asked.

"A manhole cover," Jesse said.

Everett could just make out the sides of the tunnel. They were in a little open area, a joint between the main aisleways of the culvert. On the side of the wall, Everett saw little depressions. A ladder!

Jesse started to climb.

Looking behind him, Everett could just make out the lights of the cigarette lighters. They were getting closer.

145

Harley was saying, "We got you now!"

Jesse had reached the top of the ladder. "Come on up, Everett," Jesse said. "Help me push it out."

Everett climbed up while DG waited at the bottom. Soon, both he and Jesse were pushing on the iron penny-shaped manhole cover. It was heavy. But as they pushed, a little creaking noise erupted.

"We're getting it," Jesse said, breathing hard. He put his back into it. Below him, Everett pushed with a free hand.

The manhole cover squeaked and shrieked. Then suddenly a crack of light appeared. "We got it," Jesse said.

He pushed the cover up and over. Light streamed in. Behind them, Harley screamed, "We got you now!"

Jesse climbed through. A moment later, Everett leaped out of the hole. They were in the middle of a street. But no cars came down toward them. It looked deserted. It was a part of town Everett had never seen.

"Not many cars come along here," Jesse said. "That's why I chose it."

DG hustled through the hole. They all heard Harley's voice, and looking down, his face suddenly appeared at the bottom.

"Quick. Put the cover back!" Jesse said.

They all moved the cover into place as Harley climbed. Just as he got a finger into the crack, the boys slid it into place. Harley screamed with pain.

"Now stand on it!" Jesse said. "He won't be able to move all of us."

146

All three of the kids stood on the manhole cover. A minute later, they felt someone trying to heave it off.

"Not even Harley's that strong," Jesse said, smiling.

Everett laughed. For a second, the manhole cover seemed to jostle around. But then it stopped.

"We've got them," Jesse said. "Just a few more minutes and we run."

There was more pushing on the manhole cover. But Harley and his friends couldn't budge it with three kids standing on it. Soon, the sounds underneath died away.

"Step off," Jesse said.

They all stepped off and waited. Everett watched the cover for signs of someone pushing. Nothing.

"We're safe," Jesse said. "Come on. Let's get back to the tree fort. We have to plan our next move."

As they ran, Everett kept thinking that it was only getting worse. Harley was as big a thug as ever. Would Thurston Farmer really be able to do anything? He thought of the story of Zaccheus again. Somehow he felt that held a key. But what key? What did it demonstrate that they should do?

He couldn't figure it out. The rally was one day away. In the morning they'd be putting up the stage and bringing in the sound equipment. He had to think fast. What did Zaccheus show him? He told himself it was nothing, but he couldn't shake the feeling that it meant something.

As they jogged toward the tree fort, DG suddenly said, "I know what we have to do."

"What?" Everett and Jesse said.

"Let's go get Linc and Tina. And the boats. We have to think of some defensive measures."

All three boys ran excitedly up through the woods. What was DG up to now?

16
Tricks of the Trade

In the three boats, with DG in one alone, they started up the creek. DG had put several Tupperware containers he'd heisted from his mother's kitchen into his boat. He also had a little net and four boxes with him, but he wouldn't tell anyone what he was up to.

Everett and Linc rode in the second boat, and Tina and Jesse in the other. DG led them all.

"We've got to find four of them or so," he called out to the others.

"Four of what?"

"Snappers, of course," DG said. "Defensive measures.

And maybe a few mygalomorphs."

"Mygalo-what?" Jesse asked.

"Spiders," Tina informed him. "Big ugly spiders."

They paddled up the stream until they reached the part of the creek where they'd seen the spiders.

"Look around," DG said. "Let's get about a dozen."

Everett spotted one in a web on the shore and took DG's net to capture it. Then Tina saw one, and then Jesse. Soon they had ten large ugly spiders in one of the boxes. DG punched holes in the top with his knife. "My mom never uses these anyway," he said. "She got a whole lot of them at some Tupperware party, but they just sit on the shelves. We all hate leftovers at our house."

They clambered back into the boats.

"Look for snappers, any size," DG said. "We need to capture three or four."

"What are they for?" Tina asked, twisting a long strand of hair in her fingers.

"You'll see," DG said. "Precautionary measures."

"He'll probably drop them on Harley's head or something," Linc said with glee. "That would be something—to have four snappers bite into his earlobes." He made a face, pretending to have little snapping turtles hanging from his ears.

DG just went on with his search. Everett wondered what he was up to, but when the boy wanted to keep something secret, there was no getting it out of him. They paddled slowly upcreek, dipping in their paddles gently and pulling so as not to make ripples.

Suddenly DG told everyone to be quiet. "There's a snapper sunning himself on that rock."

Everett peered into the gloomy recesses of the creek bank. He saw nothing. Then there was a splash.

"Rats! He jumped in," DG cried. "Quick! Get him as he's swimming."

Linc was the closest. He dragged the net under the water at the swimming turtle, but he came up dry.

"Follow him in the boat," DG yelled.

The snapper was perfectly visible in the clear water. He swam with a distorted frog stroke, his four feet splayed out, seeming to grab at the water.

Linc threw the net to Everett. "Catch him! He's yours!"

The net was small, really just a butterfly net, but it had a wide mouth that could be pulled shut with a lever on the handle. Everett raked through the water at the sprinting turtle. A moment later he had him. He jerked the lever, shutting the mouth of the net, and pulled the snapper up.

"Great!" DG shouted. "One down."

Everett held the small turtle up in the net and DG opened one of the containers. After punching holes in the cover, he held it out over the water. "Dump him in!" DG said.

Everett didn't want to get near those jaws. He uncinched the lever and the mouth of the net opened. Then he turned it over and dumped the turtle into the Tupperware container. The turtle scurried around on the clear plastic. DG popped the top on, and the snapper was caught permanently.

"All right, let's find two or three more," DG said.

"Are there that many around here?" Tina said, shivering a little.

Everett noticed the tremor. "Whatsa matter—scared?"

"I didn't notice you sticking your fingers in there," Tina said.

"Yeah. I'm not getting near him."

"Look around," DG said. "Look for things that look like rocks by the shore. Turtles like to bask in the sun, or just lie in shallow water and rest."

Everett took the container with the snapper in it and peered at it. The turtle had a rough back, like vertebrae sticking out. The whole shell was a mass of knobby plates. Ugly. The turtle slid around, blinking its little eyes and snapping its pincer-like mouth. He didn't look like the kind of turtle you'd write a storybook about.

"I see one!" Tina suddenly yelled. "Over there in the reeds."

A patch of reeds grew by the edge of the water. Sure enough, on a small rock sat a snapper, sunning himself. This one looked bigger than the first. And probably meaner.

DG paddled softly over toward the reeds. The turtle didn't move. Flies buzzed around their heads, and the air suddenly filled with gnats. The hunters all began flailing their arms around their heads.

"Pull back," DG said. "Wait till the cloud of gnats passes."

They fell back, but the snapper came alive, raising its head and snapping at the nearest insects.

Seconds later, the cloud passed on down the creek. DG started in again. This time he caught the snapper handily, sweeping him right up in the net before he had a chance to jump off the rock.

By mid afternoon, they had three snappers, all about the same size—about six inches from head to tip of tail. Small but deadly. DG put them in three separate containers. They also caught a few more spiders so that the fourth container was crammed full of them. A big fuzzy ball of hairy spiders.

"Come on, DG," Tina said. "What are you going to do with them? I don't want to wake up with one of those snappers in my bed."

"I wouldn't do such a thing," DG said with a grin. "Unless the bed was inhabited by someone named Harley. What I'm going to do is put a little surprise in the junction boxes for the sound system in case Harley dares to mess with them."

"Put the snappers in with all the electrical stuff?" Everett asked.

"Yeah. Harley wants to disrupt the proceedings, he'll probably go for the electricity. But he opens up one of those boxes, he'll find a surprise waiting."

"Yuck!" Tina said.

But Jesse smiled. "Harley afraid of dogs. Wonder what

he'd do with a snapper?"

"What about the spiders?" Everett asked.

"Something special for them," DG said with a wink, but he didn't explain.

They turned the boats around and floated down creek. At Linc and Tina's, they found a basket in the garage. There they stored the snappers and the spiders.

17
Morning

Saturday morning dawned clear and cool. Everett awoke with excitement already surging through his heart. By nine o'clock he, along with his dad and the other kids and parents, would be down at the park. They'd set up the stage and get the sound equipment tested. Over five hundred folding chairs had to be set up too. The rally would start at seven o'clock p.m. The police had promised to post a guard there all day and have several teams from the force there that night.

At eight-thirty he got a call from Jesse, who'd been back at his own place since school started.

"Everett, would you come with me to see my mom in the hospital?" Jesse said over the line. "She wants to meet with all of us before the rally."

There was so much to do. But this was what the rally was all about. "I'll call DG, Linc, and Tina. Anyone else?"

"No, just you guys. And Jeff Simmons, too."

"All right."

Everett called the kids and Jeff. It was all set up in a few minutes. Jeff would drive them down to the park and get things started there with the parents who were helping. Then the group would slip away to go to the hospital.

At the park, things were already in motion. Jeff had lined up a number of men from the church to put up the stage. A large area was roped off, and people from the community stood around watching. Someone arrived in a truck with speakers mounted on it. The sound system was inside. By eleven o'clock things were well in hand. More neighbors had shown up to gawk. Kids played here and there around the rope sidelines.

That morning, Tina called Thurston Farmer to make sure it was a go. He replied, "I'll be there, and possibly with a bigger surprise than you asked for."

Tina didn't ask what it was, but she reported to Everett, DG, and Jesse that things were looking better and better.

The puppies looked excellent. Their coats were shiny, and they played in their basket like pros.

Jesse said he hoped they were auctioned for at least a hundred dollars each. "That would be a real reason for pride on Queenie's part," he said. Queenie herself was done up in a red bow and looked the part of the supreme hostess.

About eleven-thirty, Jeff Simmons gathered everyone together. "If we're going to see your mom, Jesse, it better be now."

On the way to Jeff's car, though, Everett noticed Harley and his thugs hanging out on the street corner opposite the park. They didn't look happy or friendly. As the group drew near, Harley stepped into their path.

"We don't want no whities messin' with our community," he said to Jeff.

Jeff didn't flinch. "This is not a white thing or a black thing, Harley. It's for Jesse's mom. That's all it is. We're helping out because we're Christians."

Harley snorted and spit into the dirt. "You come on our turf, you deal with me!"

"This is nobody's turf," Jeff said. Jesse and DG stepped up onto either side of Jeff. "It's a public park. I hope you're not planning to disturb the events this evening."

"I do what I feel like doin'." Harley suddenly put his hand in his pocket and pulled out a knife. A second later, the silver blade flashed into the light. Harley took an apple from one of the other thugs in his band. He started peeling it, then took a large chunk and popped it into his mouth. He still hadn't moved out of Jeff's path.

"You gonna put down Thurston Farmer, too," Jesse suddenly said.

"I diss who I wanta diss," Harley hissed at Jesse. "He's an

Oreo anyway. Black on the outside but white on the inside. He's nothin.' "

"We need to get going," Jeff said. He stepped around Harley, but Harley immediately sidestepped back into his path. All the while he cut the apple into chunks and ate them.

"Let us by," Jeff said. "We're not messing with you."

"No, I'm messin' with you."

On the street, there was the sudden sound of a siren. A police car pulled up at the curb. The policeman on the shotgun side rolled down his window. "Is there a problem here?"

"No, officer," Jeff said. "We're on our way." He stepped carefully around Harley, and the kids followed. A moment later they were in the car. The policeman continued talking to Harley, but no one overheard what he said. Harley and his friends soon walked away.

"He's gonna be trouble," Jesse said. "I told you that."

"We know that," DG said. "It's taken care of."

"How?"

"You'll see. You're praying, aren't you, Everett?"

Taken by surprise, Everett looked at DG. "Well, yeah. The whole Kairo group is praying."

"Right. So God's on our side."

"And the devil's on Harley's," Jesse said. "I seen the devil beat God plenty of times."

"We'll see," DG said. "Harley doesn't have any snapping turtles."

They drove in silence to the hospital. Once there, they all went up to the fifth floor where Mrs. Hawkins's room was. Jesse led them all in, and his mother greeted them with a big smile.

"You takin' care of my boy?" she asked DG and Everett. "Don't let him get into no trouble. He's a good boy, and I don't want him mixing in that bunch that hangs around doin' nothin' but causin' trouble."

"I'm keepin' clean, Mom," Jesse said. He winked at Everett.

"Well, I want you to tell that Thurston Farmer he better make a good speech and put it on tape so I can hear it. Okay?"

"Whatever you want, Mom," Jesse said, grinning.

"Now, this is what I want to tell you all," Mrs. Hawkins said. "I'm extremely grateful for what you're doing. It's noble, it's God-honoring, and I will never forget it. But if things don't go as well as you hope, I won't be disappointed, understand?"

"Mom . . ."

"This is tough stuff, Jesse. Lots of people out there that don't want it to succeed. They against everything, and the fact that you got some white folks involved gonna make them mad. I know. I been on the receivin' end of that, too. So you go do your best, and whatever happens I'll thank the Lord for.

"And another thing . . . I know how you wanted to keep those puppies. I love Queenie too. But you come up with a good idea. An auction! Never woulda thought of that myself. I hope they all get a thousand dollars!"

"Maybe they will, Mom."

Jesse's mother smiled. "Maybe they will at that. Now come here and give your old mama a hug."

Jesse and Boop sprang forward and everyone hugged. Soon everyone was crying, and Everett's throat knotted into a lump. Then Mrs. Hawkins shooed them out. "Now you go do your thing and I'll be prayin'." She lay back on the pillow and sighed, and everyone filed out.

On the way down the hall, Jeff said to Jesse, "That's some mom you got there, Jesse."

"She okay."

"She's a winner in my book."

"Yeah," DG said. "She reminds me of my mom. My mom is always hugging and stuff like that."

"All moms are like that," Linc said.

Everyone laughed. They shambled down the hall as if they'd won the NBA championships.

At the nurses' station, a woman stopped the boys. "You the kids doing the rap rally up in New Castleton?"

"Yes," Jesse said. He nudged Everett, and they all walked over.

"Well, I want to say that's the best thing I've heard going on in this area. You are a brave bunch of kids. The president ought to call you up and congratulate you. We need kids like you." She patted Jesse on the back.

"It was their idea," he said, pointing to DG, Everett,

Linc, and Tina. "I'm just coming along."

Everett felt his face burn with a blush.

"Well, you're all doing right. Don't forget it."

They headed out of the hospital on an invisible cloud of hope. With all the compliments, Everett was sure they couldn't lose. But would it all come off? And what were Harley and his friends planning to do?

Everett kept thinking about the story of Zaccheus, and something else: he kept getting a picture of Harley and the drug man in the act. It was a crazy plan, he knew. And dangerous. He wasn't even sure he should reveal it to anyone. But he felt he shouldn't leave out DG. And yet, it might be the plan's undoing, if everyone knew about it. He decided to bide his time.

18
The Great Ones Come

After lunch, everyone went back to the park for final checks. The rap groups were taking turns using the sound stage. A crowd had gathered to listen to them.

DG took Everett aside. "All right, now we have to get our defensive measures in place." He picked up one of the Tupperware boxes with a snapper in it. "I'll do the first one. You take the second, and I'll do the third."

"What will we do with the spiders?"

"Something special."

DG opened the container. The snapper immediately clapped its jaws in frustration. "He's a mean one," DG said.

He and Everett found the sound man and told him about the problem.

"All right," the man said. "As long as you take them out afterwards."

"Done," DG said.

He and Everett crept under the sound stage and found one of the junction boxes. A lot of wire fed into it. The box provided the main link to the source of energy set up at one of the main electrical circuit boxes on the street and had a little click lock. There wasn't much space amidst the wires, but the snapper would fit in easily. In the dark, it would be nearly invisible.

"Harley tries anything with this, he's going to get snapped," DG said, twitching his eyebrows confidently. He dropped in the snapper. It landed on its back. But DG used a little stick to turn him over. "This one is Elmer."

"Elmer?" Everett said with a laugh.

"The other two are Jehoshaphat and Henrietta."

Everett laughed again. "You really know how to pick the names, don't you?"

"Turtles, especially snappers, have to have cool names, or they won't cooperate," DG explained. "I've been coaching them."

They put the other snappers in two other boxes under the stage. Then DG revealed what he planned to do with the spiders. He had them in a large trash bag. As he rigged it up under the stage where the primary sound consoles stood, he explained, "I put this line down along here. If anyone tries to come in at this point—and it's the main one—he trips the line. The bag opens, and all the spiders drop down on him. Think it'll work?"

"I don't know," Everett said with amazement. "But if it does, you'll have one scared thug on your hands."

"You got it!"

By mid afternoon everyone was raring to go. It was still two more hours till the rally, but some people had already arrived and taken up choice seats. Linc and Tina acted as ushers and seated people. Tina had made up a little bulletin which Jeff had run off at the church. She and Linc handed each new arrival a copy. On the front were pictures of Thurston Farmer, Mrs. Hawkins, and the puppies. Inside, the bulletin listed the bands in order of playing.

Most of the bands had already practiced. The stage was clear. Harley and his friends were hanging out on the corner, watching. They didn't come in and take seats. Harley kept walking around the whole area as if inspecting it. Everett longed for him to open one of those junction boxes. He could hear the scream of pain now! It would serve Harley right.

The biggest problem for Everett to figure out was where Harley and the drug man would meet. Certainly they weren't going to meet in the same place. They knew that he and Jesse and DG had heard them. So where would they meet?

Everett realized he had to let Jesse and DG know what he was doing. He couldn't go it alone. It wouldn't work. In a way he wanted to come off as the big hero of the story, but he reckoned there was room for more than one hero. And anyway, what did it matter who ended up being the hero? So long as everything worked out, he didn't care if his name was up in lights.

He finally took DG aside.

"Look," Everett said, "I've been cooking something up to capture Harley and his friends in the act." He explained his plan, and DG kept nodding as he listened.

"It might work," DG said, "if Harley does everything you think. But what if he doesn't?"

"Then we're cooked."

DG sucked his lip a moment. "What about the Zaccheus thing?"

"What Zaccheus thing?"

"You know," DG said. "Seth's story about Zaccheus— how Jesus turned him around. I thought you wanted to do that with Harley."

"I don't know whether it'll work." Everett had been thinking more and more about that. It had occurred to him that maybe Harley would change if Thurston Farmer did something like what Jesus had done. But what? Everett said, "I haven't even come up with what to do yet."

"It's simple," DG said. "When Thurston Farmer comes in, we have him go right to Harley and invite him to sit in the front. Same way Jesus invited Zaccheus to eat with him."

Everett's eyes popped open. "That may be it. Yeah! But

do you think Thurston would do it?"

"Sure," DG said. "Why not? If we remind him about Zaccheus."

Everett's mind was suddenly zooming. "What if we take a picture—a Polaroid of Thurston Farmer and Harley together, and then have Thurston sign it? And then Thurston can talk on how the community needs to come together! Maybe that would work."

"I think we should try it," DG said. "Why not? The worst it can do is fail. And maybe it'll make Harley a friend. Maybe it'll make him see the evil of what he's doing. Maybe he'll even start to be nice to Jesse."

"Sounds like some pretty big maybes."

"Yeah. But it's worth a try."

"We'll have to wait till Thurston shows up," Everett concluded. "Then we'll talk to him real quick, before he starts going through the crowd."

"Got it," DG said. "Stay on the lookout. He's supposed to show up at seven-thirty, just before the bands start. You'll have to go home and get your Polaroid camera, though."

"I already have it."

"Oh, that's right. You're going to nail Harley if he goes for the drugs."

"Right."

"Well, I'd better go with you. And Jesse too."

"We'll have to watch Harley closely. He'll probably still meet with the drug man during the rally, even if Thurston Farmer talks to him."

"Yeah, we'll both watch. I'll tell Jesse," DG said. "Keep your fingers crossed."

Everett went back to check on his camera. He had it stored in his little backpack at Jesse's apartment. The camera was all ready to go. He had three packs of film, thirty-six exposures. Surely that was enough to do all he planned to do that night.

As time wore on, Everett's anxiety increased. He was sweating, and his fingers shook a little. He walked around the park several times to calm down. More and more people were showing up. He just wished it would all start. He hated playing the waiting game.

At the same time, he kept on the lookout. Harley continued his forays around the park. He didn't try anything that Everett could see, but he was probably just biding his time. Everett prayed that the Zaccheus idea would work. If it didn't affect Harley, he prayed it would influence the other gang members. Surely they would be amazed and honored to have personal pictures signed by Thurston Farmer. If they heard his testimony, maybe they'd even become Christians. Everett thought that was a long shot. But why not hope for that? It happened all the time in the world. People were changed because they trusted Christ. It had happened to him, Everett Abels, when he'd become a Christian. Why couldn't it happen here?

He walked around with the camera hanging from a strap around his neck, but he didn't take any pictures. He wanted to conserve as much film as possible. The flash attachment was in his backpack. As it got darker, he'd need that.

It was seven o'clock. The seats had filled up. Excitement cut the air. Kids ran this and that way. Little ones. Older ones. They were all over the place. Everyone was talking about Thurston Farmer, the puppies, and Mrs. Hawkins. Everett was pleased. It couldn't have been better.

It was as Everett and DG were walking around the back of the stage that a sudden scream broke the air. They heard a loud bump and another scream.

It came from under the stage!

Everett ducked down. Immediately, he saw Harley under there. He had opened a junction box. The snapper had gotten him.

Harley shook the snapper off his hand. People ran from different directions to see what had happened. Harley simply walked out. When he saw DG and Everett, he said, "I know you guys did this. You're dead meat. Understand? Dead meat!"

He stalked by. People shouted to him, "What's the matter, Harley? Couldn't do your dirty work?"

Harley simply sneered and found the rest of his gang. Everett overheard him say, "The thing was booby-trapped!"

Then another scream broke on the air. One of Harley's thugs ran out screaming, "They're all over me!" It was the spiders! They'd done their job too.

Everett just smiled. Well, at least DG's plan had worked. Harley and his cohorts would stay away from the stage from now on.

DG crept back under the stage and caught the scurrying turtle. He said to Everett, "We'll put him back in his little box for now. Take him back to the creek later."

Everett slapped DG on the back. "Looks like your plan worked."

"Yeah, now let's see if yours does."

They both stepped out from under the stage. Something was happening. The crowd was cheering. Everett and DG ran toward the street. Jesse was there to catch them.

"It's Thurston Farmer!" Jesse cried. "He's here. And he brought a bunch of 76ers with him—including the whole starting line-up!"

"Yo!" DG said, shooting his hand into the air.

Everett gave him a shove. "Come on, we have to tell Thurston our plan."

19
The Team

Thurston Farmer immediately liked the Zaccheus plan. "That's a great idea, guys," he said to Jesse, Everett, and DG. Linc and Tina and Boop ran up a second later. "Just point them out to me and let's do it."

Harley and his friends had spread out in the crowd. DG was the first to spot one of them. As Thurston and the other 76ers plodded down the middle aisle, they shook hands with people and embraced the ladies. The eight men towered over everyone. It was a majestic moment.

"There's one," DG said. He ran over to one of the gang members. "Wait here," he said. "Thurston wants to meet you." At first the boy scowled, but when Thurston Farmer and the others walked over, his jaw dropped.

"We want to get a picture," Everett shouted. "Stand there."

He motioned to the men to stand around the gang member. His name was Richie. After the photo slid out of the camera, Thurston and the others signed it on the back.

"Come up and sit up front," Thurston said with a wink at Everett.

It went that way for the next fifteen minutes. Thurston posed with each of the gang members and many others. Everett was soon down to his last packet of film.

Then Everett saw Harley. He had been watching from the sidelines. "There he is," Everett whispered to Thurston, trying not to look like he was looking. "What are you going to do?"

Thurston just said, "You watch."

He and the other 76ers went right for the gang leader. A moment later, Thurston hoisted him to two of their shoulders. With Harley half on one shoulder and half on the second player's, Everett snapped the photo. Harley looked dazed.

"I never had nothin' like this," he said.

"Well, come on up to the front," Thurston said with a big grin. "You're an honored guest here."

By now Thurston had invited so many people besides gang members to sit up front that the men were scrambling to put in a new row of chairs. Some of the people in the former first row complained, but it turned out all right. All the gang members sat together with Jesse and the rest of the kids. Everett's parents and family were in the crowd too. So were Linc and Tina's, and DG's. A lot of people from the church had shown up too. And Seth and Mr. Hennessee, minus their dogs. It was a party atmosphere.

Then DG, who had been nominated master of ceremonies, started it off. The rap groups began their tunes, and soon everyone was moving to the beat. DG cracked jokes and did a masterful job between set-ups. All the while, Everett watched Harley to see if he would disappear into the crowd. But Harley stayed still, riveted to the program.

DG explained about how this was a fund-raiser for Mrs. Hawkins. He told a little about the lady between bands. Then he explained about the puppies and held them up. "These three little doggies are going to be auctioned off," DG intoned, "to the highest bidder. All the proceeds go to the Mrs. Hawkins fund."

There was loud cheering all the way through.

By nine o'clock all the rap groups had played. The winner would be announced after Thurston spoke. DG told a couple more jokes, and the crowd kept laughing.

Then Thurston Farmer took the stage. He opened with some comments about basketball and how he appreciated the community support of the 76ers. Then he launched into his testimony. He had become a Christian as a kid in his teens. Friends had gotten him involved in a gang. The gang was into some bad things: drugs and stealing.

"Then one day," Thurston said, "this old guy started coming into the community. He met with us kids. Played ball with us. Checkers and chess. I was good at chess. He started telling us about this person, Jesus. Most of my friends knew about Jesus, and they thought it was a laugh. But something about the way the man talked held me. I wanted to hear more.

"After weeks of this, I finally decided I wanted to follow Jesus. It was that simple. So I prayed, and the old man—whose name was Ray Rivers—prayed with me. Ever since then my life has been three things: Jesus, my family, and basketball, in that order. I got away from the gang and got into organized sports. Learned my first moves in high school, playing for a team in Newark, New Jersey. I went on to UCLA, as you all know, and played for one of the best collegiate teams that ever existed. It's been a good life."

Everett noticed that DG was listening intently as Thurston spoke. So were the gang members. Harley had his eyes fixed on the tall basketball player as if there was no one else in the whole place. Everett prayed that when Thurston gave an invitation, if he did, that they would all become Christians.

Thurston concluded his talk, "If you want to follow Jesus, it's simple. Just tell Him that. Talk to Him in prayer. He's there, listening and waiting. Tell Him you want to leave your sins behind and become a new person. Ask Him to come in and be the master of your life. And tell Him that you want to be forgiven for everything. I bid you to do that tonight. No one knows what tomorrow may bring. But if you seal it tonight, it'll last through all eternity."

Finally, Thurston bowed his head and led the whole crowd in prayer. Everett bowed and prayed with them. He hoped DG, Linc and Tina, and Jesse and Boop would be among those who prayed to become Christians. But he told himself not to be disappointed if they didn't. There would be other opportunities.

When Thurston finished, he looked up, and DG took the stage again. DG said, "I hope you all took this man seriously, because I did, and I'm Jewish."

There was loud clapping, and Everett wondered what DG meant. Then he noticed something: Harley was gone.

20
Private Eyes

Jesse grabbed Everett's arm. "Come on, I saw him go out the side. Let's see if we can catch up."

Everett's heart sank. He had hoped Harley had really changed, but it looked as though he hadn't.

They crept, low to the ground, out from the front row. People looked at them questioningly, but they kept going.

A moment later, when they reached the street, Jesse pointed. "There he is."

Harley loped up the south side of the street. He hadn't turned into the woods yet, so Everett thought they might catch him. Maybe they could even persuade him not to meet with the drug man.

They both ran across the street. Everett still had his camera. There were six shots left. Harley slowed down, and as Everett and Jesse drew nearer, they noticed him whistling. That was strange, Everett thought. They kept to the shadows, but if Harley turned around, he'd see them both right away.

A moment later, the cyclone fence gate in front of one of the houses creaked. Harley opened it and walked up the concrete path. He went to the door and opened it.

Everett and Jesse looked at one another. "What's he doing?" Everett asked.

"I don't know," Jesse said, "That's his house. Let's go around back. Maybe he's gonna go out the back door and head for the woods from there."

They hurried around back and hid in some bushes. No one appeared at the door. They waited for several minutes, then decided it was a lost cause.

Then a light came on.

A second later, the door opened. Harley pushed open the screen and stood in the doorway. In the light, he looked big and mean.

Everett barely dared to breathe.

Then Harley said, "Oh, boys, are you there?"

Everett glanced at Jesse uneasily. Did Harley know they were there?

"Oh, boys," Harley said in a falsetto, mocking voice. "Are you looking for me?"

Still Everett and Jesse said nothing.

Finally Harley walked down the steps. "I got to come and whisk you guys out of the bushes or somethin'?"

He was too close. Everett stood up. "We're here."

Harley grinned. "That's better. What are you doin', followin' me around? You want to get another beatin'?"

Jesse said, "We thought you were going to meet with the drug man."

Harley let his head fall back, and he laughed. "You thought I was going to meet with him, huh? You heard me last night. You think we were going to meet after you'd found out? What, you think we're dumb?"

"Then what were you doing?" Everett asked sheepishly.

Harley laughed. "I came home to use the toilet, for your information." He snorted with sarcasm. "This beats all. Can't even go to the bathroom without bein' suspected. I ought to box your two heads together."

Everett felt embarrassed and ridiculed.

Harley turned to go back inside. He said in a falsetto, still mocking tone, "See you back at the rally, boys."

Everett didn't know what to think of it. Harley hadn't been too mean. But had he changed? For real?

For now it was a mystery. But at least he hadn't met with the drug leader. So that was a change, and for the better.

Jesse and Everett slunk off back to the street and then ran all the way back to the rally. They arrived to see DG begin auctioning off the dogs. Each of them went for about a hundred dollars. Then the pastors of several of the churches spoke. Plates were passed, and people donated to the fund.

Finally, the winners of the rap contest were announced. Thurston and his fellow players invited everyone to come to a 76ers game, and things wound down to the conclusion. Harley didn't come back, but after the rally, the other members of his gang were friendly. None of them gave any threatening scowls, and one told Jesse that he'd decided to become a Christian like Thurston. They all proudly displayed their pictures.

Everett and the others stayed for the clean-up. DG removed the snappers from their junction boxes and lamented that the spiders had all gotten away. "I was hoping to use them in a horror movie I'm gonna film," he said with a laugh.

They all went down to the creek and let the snappers go.

Working hard, everything was put away by twelve. It had been an exhausting day. And for Everett there was church in the morning. He wished his mom and dad would just sleep in.

The kids all promised to meet the next afternoon. They wanted to visit Mrs. Hawkins in the hospital and tell her all that had happened.

Harley didn't come back to the rally, though. Everett wondered if he'd outfoxed them and gone to meet with the drug man anyway. There was nothing he could do about it, so he decided just to leave that in God's hands.

At twelve-ten, Jesse slapped everyone's hands. The ministers would be presenting Mrs. Hawkins with a check the next day in a little ceremony. Over four thousand dollars had been raised.

Jeff gave the other kids a ride home.

"It was a great rally," Tina said. "DG, you were fantastic."

DG gave a sheepish grin.

Everett suggested that he would grow up and become a comedian, but DG said, "No, not until I've found a cure for cancer."

With that, Jeff let DG off at his house and drove down toward Linc and Tina's.

21
Change and No Change

Jesse and Boop boarded the two little boats.

"We'll go up to the tree fort," DG explained, "and have a little party. Celebrate."

They had all visited Mrs. Hawkins that afternoon in the hospital. She was grateful for the raised money and the love of so many.

"You kids done an amazing thing," she said with tears in her eyes. "I'm so happy." She hugged them all.

It was now about four o'clock Sunday afternoon. The kids had come down in the boats. It was probably the last jaunt they could take on the creek. The weather was already getting cooler.

They started up the creek. No one had seen any signs of the snappers since DG let them off in the creek the night before. "They've probably gone home," Everett said, watching the water as they paddled. "They still give me the shivers."

"Well, it looks like Harley's gonna be a different person," Tina said. She was in the boat with Linc. DG had Boop, and Jesse was with Everett. They'd left Queenie at home with Michael, the pup that Boop had kept.

"Maybe," DG said. "I'd be surprised though."

Everett said, "What did you mean last night, DG, when you said you hoped everyone took Thurston Farmer seriously?"

"Just that," DG said. "He was serious, so I was serious."

"You didn't pray the prayer, though, did you?" Everett asked. His heart suddenly began pounding.

"Sort of," DG answered, smiling slyly. "A Jewish version of it."

"Oh, you left Jesus out," Tina said.

"No," DG said. "I said, 'If you're really God, Jesus, then I want you to show me.' That's all I said. I figure if He's going to show me, He'll have to work that part out."

Everett smiled. If there was one thing he was sure of, it was that God could do far more than DG thought. But he said nothing.

They paddled along quietly. For a while no one talked. It was nice just enjoying the sun and the water. Everett saw a fish swimming, but he let it pass on down the creek. It was a sucker, anyway. Not the kind of fish anyone would want to catch and eat.

They had almost reached the overpass when suddenly they all heard voices. DG was in the lead. He held up his hand for everyone to be quiet. The boats floated silently with the current. Insects buzzed in the air.

Everett strained to hear where the voices were coming from. They seemed to come from the woods, just down from the culvert.

"This time it'll work," a voice said. It sounded familiar. "They all probably think I'm converted."

"Good," said another lower voice. "But you have to unload it fast."

"I will."

"It's Harley," DG said suddenly. "I recognize the voice." He pointed to shore. "Let's beach the boats."

Everett had his camera with him again. He had planned to use up the last pictures at the tree fort. But now his heart sank. Harley had been playing a game. He hadn't changed at all. Well, then, this time they'd nail him.

The boats ran aground and everyone climbed out silently. After pulling the boats up and tying them together, the kids clambered up the bank. The voices kept talking. They were just on this side of the overpass, up in the trees.

DG led them. "Keep quiet," he whispered. "Ev, you got the camera ready?"

"Ready."

"Linc," DG said. "You stay here with the boats. Tina and Boop should stay with you."

"I want to go," Linc said angrily.

"We can't all go," DG said. "And it's important. Whenever King David fought and left men with the baggage, they all got an equal reward."

"So what's that have to do with it?"

Everett looked at Tina. "Would you stay with Boop? If anything happens, we don't want her getting caught."

Tina nodded. "Linc, you go. I'll be all right. We'll hide right down under the bank."

"Hurry," DG said.

The four boys crept through the weeds and undergrowth. Everyone kept down, ducking low. There were plenty of trees for cover. The boys crawled up behind a log. There in the trees stood Harley, two of his gang members, and the drug man. The tall man held a bag slung over his shoulder. He opened it and began showing Harley what was inside.

DG whispered, "Will the camera make much noise?"

Everett nodded. "I think they could hear me."

"Take the picture while one is talking," he said.

"I don't know," Everett said. "It can be loud."

"We have to get a picture."

"Then get ready to run!" Everett said anxiously.

"We'll be ready."

Rising off the ground, Everett aimed the camera. His heart thumped. The drug man was talking and showing

Harley the things in the bag. Everyone stood stooped over, looking inside.

Everett pushed the shutter button. A little winding sound erupted. It sounded like a gun going off in the quiet.

Immediately, Harley and the others jumped. They all turned around. "What was that?" Harley yelled.

"Don't tell me you got more people lookin' at us?" the drug man yelled.

"Over there," one of the gang members cried. "They got a camera."

"Go!" DG shouted.

All four of the boys hit it. Everett knew immediately they couldn't go back to the boats. Why hadn't they thought about this before? Why did the camera have to make so much noise? What idiots they were!

They sprinted through the trees toward the creek.

"Up to the underpass," DG yelled. He was out ahead of everyone. Harley, his two friends, and the drug man all followed in eager pursuit.

"We gotta get that camera," yelled the adult thug.

They were all bigger than the kids, but maybe not as fast. Everett's sneakers slapped on the concrete of the flat part under the highway bridge.

"Into the tunnel!" Jesse yelled.

"No!" DG answered. "They might cut us off. Let's go up the trail."

They were breathing hard.

The trail wound around the edges of the creek. There

was nowhere to hide. How far would the thugs chase them? It looked as if they weren't going to stop.

Everett thought briefly of making it to the tree fort, but that was pretty far away.

Then up ahead Everett spotted the cattails. Maybe they could hide in them!

But four of them? No way. The cattails were too smashed down.

Everett ran at the head of the group. "Where to?" he yelled. He glanced behind just long enough to see Harley coming around the last bend. He was running hard too. And this time he had a knife in his hand. The silver blade glinted in the sunlight.

"What have we gotten ourselves into?" Everett murmured as he pumped his feet harder. He was running out of reserve power. Looking behind him, he could see that Jesse and Linc had run out of steam too. They both looked sick. DG, though, looked as if he could run another mile no sweat.

Everett hit the cattails. The long fronds swished against his legs and arms. Then it hit him: Mr. Hennessee and the dogs!

Everett called out behind him. "Up the hill to the barn!"

"Yeah!" DG answered. "Come on."

22
Help!

The hill was murder. Everett's lungs felt as if they would burst in half. "Charlie," he wheezed. "Jasper! Bunk! Duke! All of you!"

There was no sound of barking. Where were they?

He skidded up over the crest of the hill. Behind him, DG almost ran into his back. Jesse was fifty feet behind, and Linc farther. The drug man, Harley, and the others were catching up.

"Hurry, Linc!" Everett yelled.

Where were the dogs?

Everett ran past the little pond toward the barn.

Immediately, a dog jumped up and barked. Then all of them were on their feet.

The dogs all rushed up to greet him. Duke was first, followed by twenty-six others. As they came over the crest of the hill, the dogs spotted the intruders. Everett pointed. "Go get 'em!"

The dogs streamed down over the edge of the hill. Harley and his friends were well past the cattails now. All four of the intruders stopped in their tracks as the dogs poured down toward them.

"Get Mr. Hennessee!" Everett yelled to DG. In a second, DG was off, up past the barn to the house.

Everett stood and watched as the dogs barked and bared their teeth and formed a circle around the thugs. Linc and Jesse panted hard next to Everett on the hill.

"Good idea," Linc wheezed.

"I never woulda thought of it," Jesse said.

Moments later, Tina and Boop came out of the cattails down behind them. The dogs let them pass; they were too busy keeping their quarry under control. Several of the dogs snapped at Harley and his gang, who looked terrified. Harley huddled with the others in the middle, not trying to escape.

DG came across the barnyard with Mr. Hennessee. The old man was carrying his shotgun. "What is it, boys?"

"A drug dealer and his friends," Everett said.

Mr. Hennessee came over the hill and walked down toward the dogs and four hapless prisoners. DG, Everett,

Jesse, Linc, Boop, and Tina all walked along behind him.

"What have we here?" he asked the man with the drugs.

"Call off your dogs!" Harley shouted. It sounded more like a terrified bleat.

"Not until the police get here," Mr. Hennessee said. He instructed Linc and Tina to run up to the house and call 911. Then he leveled the shotgun on the four thugs.

"Do you know that you're trespassing?" he said.

"Then what about them?" Harley yelled.

"They're friends," Mr. Hennessee said and winked.

"Why didn't you listen to Thurston Farmer?" Jesse suddenly said to Harley and the other two boys.

"Thurston Farmer don't know what it's like," Harley sneered.

"Sure he does," Jesse said. "He wanted to help you, keep you from this."

"No, he didn't. He just wanted to make a buck."

"He didn't get paid to come to that rally," Everett answered. "He came because we asked him."

"He came because he figured it'd make him look big!" Harley growled.

"He came because he wanted to help my mom!" Jesse said, moving forward to the edge of the circle of dogs.

"You can throw that knife out here," Mr. Hennessee said to Harley. He cocked the shotgun.

Harley pitched the knife out onto the dirt. "They aren't goin' to do nothin' to us," Harley said.

"We'll see about that," Mr. Hennessee said. "Drugs are

191

serious business."

"They put you in jail for a day and then they let you out," Harley said with sarcasm. "It's an open door. I'll be out on the street tomorrow."

The drug dealer remained silent. He seemed to be studying Mr. Hennessee and looking for a way of escape. He didn't move, though, and appeared to be biding his time.

Ten minutes later a black-and-white police car pulled into the barn area. DG and Linc met the two policemen and led them down the hill.

In another five minutes, the policemen had Harley and the drug dealer in handcuffs. They marched the four of them up the hill.

"Good work," the policemen said. "We've been trying to catch this guy"—he pointed to the drug dealer—"for some time. He's been going into communities all over and getting little kids hooked."

The policemen asked Mr. Hennessee and the kids to come down to the station to make a statement. Mr. Hennessee piled everyone into his car and they took off. At the station, another officer took statements from each of the kids.

In an hour they were back at the farm, and Mr. Hennessee sent them off down the creek. "Be careful, kids," he said. "I might not be here next time."

"There won't be a next time," Jesse said. "It's over."

Everett walked up beside him. "What's the matter?" he asked.

"I thought it would end up different," he said. "With Thurston Farmer and all."

"Even Jesus didn't convert everyone," Everett said.

DG spoke up behind them. "Some people fake it too. To get what they want."

Jesse whipped around. "Are you faking it, DG?"

DG was taken aback. He said, "How can I be faking it? I haven't done anything yet."

"That's what I mean," Jesse said. "You haven't done anything, and neither has anyone else. The whole rally was a bust."

"No, it wasn't," Everett insisted. "We raised some money for your mom. Everyone had a good time. And we met the 76ers. What more could we ask for?"

"I wanted the community to be changed," Jesse said. "To get rid of all the drugs and stuff. To make it clean."

"Maybe it doesn't happen like that," DG said.

They walked on in silence past the overpass, following the trail back down to the boats. Jesse and Boop stood on the bank.

Everett said, "Why don't you come to our Kairo meeting tonight, Jesse? It might make you feel better."

"I don't think so," he said.

Everett nodded. "It's okay. You don't have to. But we were going to celebrate. A lot of kids came to the rally and had a real good time. We're going to have a party."

"Maybe I'll come," DG said.

"Us too," Tina said, glancing at Linc.

"I hope you all come," Everett said. "Even Boop. They'll let her come, even if she's not in sixth grade yet."

"We'll see," Jesse said. "What time is it?"

"Seven-thirty. At our church."

He turned to go.

The kids piled into the boats and started up the creek. Everyone was quiet for most of the trip.

When they all got out at Tina and Linc's backyard, Tina said, "I sure wish Jesse would feel better."

"I wish I would feel better," Everett said.

"Don't tell me you're depressed too," Tina commented, looking into Everett's eyes.

"I thought with Thurston Farmer, people would really change."

Tina patted Everett on the back. "Thurston Farmer's just a man," she said. "He can't do miracles."

"Yeah, I guess."

They all went to their homes. Everett felt tired and worn down. He wished things were different, but he knew there wasn't a whole lot he could do.

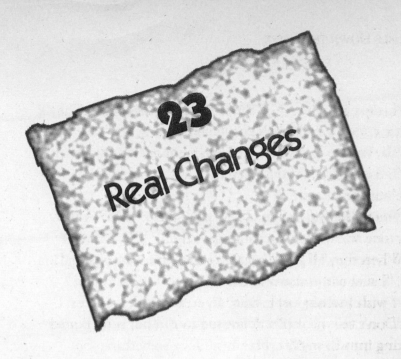

23
Real Changes

The room pulsated with excitement. Already, more kids had shown up for the celebration at church than had ever come to Kairo before. Everett recognized a lot of kids from the rally. There were blacks and whites, Asians and Hispanics. He was amazed. Thurston Farmer didn't come, but that was all right. He'd already done his job.

Everett sat with Linc and Tina and DG in the back. He wanted to let the excitement fill him, but somehow it stayed out of his heart. Then he saw Jesse and Boop step into the big gym where they were meeting.

Immediately, he and the others ran over to Jesse, greeting him.

As they sat down in the bleachers, Jeff started the meeting. "We've all just had a great event in the life of this church. I'd like to give each of you a chance to tell how it affected you, if you want. Anyone want to come to the mike and get us started?"

No one moved at first. Then a tall black girl Everett didn't know came to the podium. "I didn't know anyone cared anymore," the girl began. "I thought everyone had forgotten about us down in the Projects. But last night proved to me that people do care. And that Jesus cares. I think I became a Christian last night. I'm not sure. But for the first time in my life, I really believe something. So thanks."

There were tears in her eyes as she sat down. Everett was amazed. He hadn't expected this at all.

Then another boy, one Everett knew from Kairo, walked up. "I was really excited to hear Thurston Farmer speak," the boy said, "but I didn't consider what he would talk about. After he spoke last night, I made a decision to follow Jesus. I hadn't made that decision before, even though I come to Kairo because it's fun. But now it has real meaning for me."

Other kids stood and spoke of how they'd been changed. Everett had tears in his eyes as he listened. Here he'd been concentrating on just one person, Harley, and all these others had been greatly affected. It was wonderful.

As kid after kid went up and shared their stories, a lump formed in Everett's throat. Maybe God had worked after all, though not the way he'd prayed or expected. Maybe that was the way with God.

Suddenly Tina nudged him. "I'm going up," she said.

"You!" Everett answered.

"Yeah, me!" Tina said. She stood and walked up to the mike.

Tina wove her fingers nervously together in front of her as she looked out over the group. "Today we had quite an experience," she said. "One of the people we were hoping would change because of the rally was an older boy named Harley. He's up at the jail now because he wouldn't give up dealing drugs. I'm real sorry Harley didn't change. And I know some people are really disappointed about that.

"But I have to say this. When I heard Thurston Farmer talk about Jesus, something happened in my heart. I don't know what it was, but at that moment, I wanted to be like Jesus. I wanted to follow Him. So when Thurston Farmer prayed, I prayed with him. And I guess I became a follower of Jesus I don't know how my family's going to take that. We aren't exactly religious or anything. But I feel so full of love and hope now. God really changed me, I know. And even if He didn't change everyone we hoped, I know that what happened to me is real. And for that, I'm very happy."

Tina started to walk away. Then she turned and walked back to the mike. "And if you think that was easy for me," she said. "You're crazy. Because ever since I've known Everett Abels, I always thought his religious stuff was a little crazy. But now I know the truth. So thanks again."

Everyone seemed struck dumb after that. But then with sudden power, a cheer went up and everyone stood to their feet to shout praises to God. Even Everett joined them.

Then Jeff took the mike again. "The kids who got this rally going are all here tonight. Besides Tina, there's Everett, DG, Linc, Jeff, and Boop—er, Deanna. Please come up here."

The others filed up next to Tina as the crowd clapped and cheered. Everett felt a little embarrassed. Jeff spoke of their hard work, how the idea had come about, and how the church had gotten involved. He said, "All it takes is one person with an idea, and that one person can change the world. That's what we've seen tonight."

He shook hands with each of the kids. Then he said, "And now we have a special surprise." He motioned to the far door.

A second later it opened and a wheelchair was pushed in. In it sat Mrs. Hawkins, beaming at the kids! She was wheeled to the front, and all the kids crowded around.

"I didn't know you were gonna be here, Mom!" Jesse cried.

Boop gave her a hug and kiss.

"I had to come and thank all these grand folks," Mrs. Hawkins said. She was wheeled up to the microphone. "I don't know what to say to you all," she said. There were tears in her eyes. "But you have done a wondrous thing. And I can't help but thank you from the bottom of my heart. I'm doing better. And pretty soon, they say, they may have a donor for a transplant. So you all just keep prayin' and hopin' because our good Lord is going to do something amazing."

Everyone cheered and clapped, and Jeff invited the crowd to have some refreshments.

As Everett walked over with the others to get some punch, Tina walked up to him.

"Well, what did you think of that, Everett Abels?" she asked.

"I was amazed," Everett said.

"Well, don't be. Linc's thinking about it too. And so is DG. I can tell."

Everett looked into her eyes. "You really think so?"

"I do. You've really helped us, Evvie."

"But how?"

"Just by being you. Now I'm having a cookie. What about you?"

"Yeah."

Everett ate and thought and ate and thought. As he looked at the shining faces of the kids filing past the table, a lump hardened in his throat. Maybe God was doing more than he thought. And maybe He was planning to do even more.

He decided he could look forward to that.

Adventure at Rocky Creek

"Just give me another chance."

That's all Everett wanted—another chance to be Chuck's friend. To prove he wasn't the yellow belly coward Chuck said he was. But Chuck and his crowd weren't about to give Everett a chance to prove anything.

A long, lonely summer stretched ahead of Everett without any friends. Then he met DG, and they met Linc and Tina—plus Set and his dogs! A lonely summer turned into a pretty good one, including exploring Rocky Creek and making a rope swing to reach the other bank. Still, Everett couldn't forget Chuck and his taunt: YELLOW BELLY!

His mom said pray. The Lord would work it out. Well, he didn't see the Lord doing much of anything. Did He even care about Everett?

But one day at the abandoned house across Rocky Creek, Everett would get his second chance, and a chance to know God did care about him. Would he be able to prove to his friends and himself he wasn't a coward? Or would he blow it again?

Mark Littleton has published over a dozen books and 400 articles for youth and adults. Mark was born in New Jersey, just like Everett, but he now lives in Maryland.

Chariot Books
A Division of Cook Communications

Tree Fort Wars

"Out of control!"

Building the tree fort near Rocky Creek with DG, Linc, and Tina is the most fun Everett can remember. Why does Chuck have to spoil it?

Chuck's prejudice against DG has escalated from annoying to mean and hateful. All the attempts at peacemaking that Everett and the others try have failed. What's worse, now DG is ready to fight back at Chuck and his gang. Everett knows that a fight won't solve anything—and someone could get hurt.

He knows he should pray about it, and he does. But does God hear him when he asks, "Show me what to do"?

Finally one day at the fort, the answer comes in a surprising way—one that no one will ever forget.

Mark Littleton has published over a dozen books and 400 articles for youth and adults. Mark was born in New Jersey, just like Everett, but he now lives in Maryland.

Chariot Books
A Division of Cook Communications

Storm Wind

"I'm not going!"

The war had always been distant—nothing but newscast reports or stories from men home on leave. But now that the war is getting closer, Randal's mother is sending him to Altir—which is supposed to be safer—but he does not want to go. Determined that Altir will be boring and he'll detest his cousin, Randal quickly discovers that his expectations are anything but reality. He and his cousin Veryan soon find themselves far more involved in the fallout of the war than they ever dreamed they would be.

As the two journey through the city filled with destruction, Randal is faced with more decisions than he's faced in his life, one of which is the biggest decision he'll ever make—whether or not to take God seriously.

Visit a time when the Six Worlds were young, before their people lost contact with Earth, before the Black Years began, before it was dangerous to believe.

Cherith Baldry is involved with literature, especially children's books, in all aspects of her life. She is a teacher and school librarian and has two children of her own. She and her family live in England where she enjoys writing, reading, and gardening.

Chariot Books™
A Division of Cook Communications

Cradoc's Quest

"Life must be more than this."

Legend tells of a Book and a belief that the ancestors from Earth once held. It's an almost-forgotten belief—until now. For reasons unknown to him, Cradoc—a young farmhand who longs for something more from life—is chosen to bring that belief back to the people of the Six Worlds.

Cradoc discovers a copy of the Book, thought to have been destroyed during the Black Years. It contains truths that could cause the greatest upheaval in the history of the Six Worlds. Cradoc must get the Book to a printer so its truths may be widely read, but there are many who will try to stop him—and destroy the Book—along the way.

The people of the Six Worlds long ago lost contact with Earth and the belief of its people. Journey through the Saga of the Six Worlds and discover, as they do, that what's gone may not always be for good.

Cherith Baldry is involved with literature, especially children's books, in all aspects of her life. She is a teacher and school librarian and has two children of her own. She and her family live in England where she enjoyes writing, reading, and gardening.

Chariot Books™
A Division of Cook Communications

Rite of Brotherhood

"You must do what you can to stop this war."

Aurion leaves his home on Two Islands as a hostage of the Tar-Askans, but he also goes to Tar-Askar as an ambassador.

The people of Tar-Askar have long-ago forsaken the ways of the peace-loving God of their ancestors, and now worship the god of power and war, Askar. Aurion is convinced that the way to prevent the war the Tar-Askans are preparing for is to turn them back to worshiping God. He plans to start with Arax, the king's son and his distant cousin. When he meets Arax, however, he wonders just how wise a choice he made.

The people of the Six Worlds long ago lost contact with Earth and the belief of its people. Journey through the Saga of the Six Worlds and discover, as they do, that what's gone may not always be for good.

Cherith Baldry is involved with literature, especially children's books, in all aspects of her life. She is a teacher and school librarian and has two children of her own. She and her family live in England where she enjoys writing, reading, and gardening.

Chariot Books™
A Division of Cook Communications

◆ PARENTS ◆

Are you looking for fun ways to bring the Bible to life in the lives of your children?

Chariot Family Publishing has hundreds of books, toys, games, and videos that help teach your children the Bible and apply it to their everyday lives.

Look for these educational, inspirational, and fun products at your local Christian bookstore.